REEDICK O

REELING

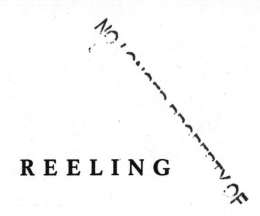

Lola Lafon

REELING

*Translated from the French
by Hildegarde Serle*

Europa
editions

Europa Editions
1 Penn Plaza, Suite 6282
New York, N.Y. 10019
www.europaeditions.com
info@europaeditions.com

Copyright © Actes Sud 2020
Published by special arrangement with Actes Sud
in conjunction with their duly appointed agent 2 Seas Literary Agency
First Publication 2022 by Europa Editions

Translation by Hildegarde Serle
Original title: *Chavirer*
Translation copyright © 2022 by Europa Editions

Library of Congress Cataloging in Publication Data is available
ISBN 978-1-60945-731-0

Lafon, Lola
Reeling

Book design by Emanuele Ragnisco
www.mekkanografici.com

Cover photo @ Elena Kulikova

Prepress by Grafica Punto Print – Rome

Printed in Italy

Forgiveness, if there is any, must only, and can only, forgive the unforgivable, the inexpiable—and thus do the impossible.
—JACQUES DERRIDA, "To Forgive"

In the absence of forgiveness, let oblivion come.
—ALFRED DE MUSSET, "October Night"

Those reasons that make our reasons futile.
Those things deep inside that keep us awake late.
—JEAN-JACQUES GOLDMAN, "Awake Late"

REELING

1

S he'd lived through so many scene changes, appearances, a life of endless nights and fresh starts. She knew all about reinvention. She knew the backstages of so many theaters, their woody smell, those winding corridors in which dancers jostled, the tired pink walls and faded linoleum of windowless dressing rooms, those mirrors framed with light bulbs, the tables on which a dresser would lay out her costume with, pinned to it, a label: CLÉO.

A cream-colored G-string, a pair of nude tights for under the fishnets, a sequin-and-pearl-covered bra, the elbow-length ivory gloves, and the high-heeled sandals reinforced with coral elastic at the instep.

Cléo would arrive before the others; she liked that time when there wasn't yet anyone fussing around her. That still silence, barely disturbed by the voices of the technicians checking the stage lighting. She'd take off her street clothes, pull on some sweatpants, and then, sitting topless in front of the mirror, would start the process that would see her disappear.

Half an hour to erase herself: she'd pour Porcelain 0.1 foundation into her cupped hand, soak a latex sponge with it. Its beige tint eliminated the pink of her lips, the flickering mauve of the eyelids, the freckles high on her cheeks, the small veins on the wrists, the scar from her appendicitis surgery, the birthmark on her thigh, a beauty spot on the left breast. For her back and bottom, help was needed from another dancer.

The hair-and-makeup artist would come by at 6 P.M., his belt-bag stuffed with brushes. He'd re-powder the forehead of one, apply concealer to the pimple of another, correct some shaky eyeliner. His calm, minty breath caressed cheeks, the rubbery sound of the gum he always chewed served as a lullaby, and the girls dozed in a hairspray haze. By 7 P.M., Cléo's nocturnal face was that of all the other dancers: an anonymous woman with false eyelashes, supplied by the establishment, cheeks flushed with fuchsia, eyes fiercely enlarged with black liner, and a pearly shimmer from cheekbone to eyebrow arch.

Cléo had stood behind dozens of red-velvet drapes, curtains, felt hangings; she'd been through this same ritual hundreds of times, these incantatory checks: shaking the head from right to left to test the hold of the hair, jumping in place to keep the thigh muscles warm while awaiting the stage manager's signal, that 4-3-2-1 countdown. The dressers fastened, tweaked, secured, one last time, the requisite feathered headdress, that deceptive crown of softness, its support gripping the shoulder blades like an iron backpack.

Cléo and the others liked to gauge the audience from behind the curtain, interpreting the slightest sneeze or throat clearing: *guess they're on edge tonight.*

Barely out of their coaches—they came from Dijon, Rodez, the airport—they found their seats like overexcited schoolkids, dazzled by the reflections from the crystal glasses on their table and the brass champagne buckets. They marveled at the white rose in its translucent vase, the attentiveness of the waiters, the red banquettes and white tablecloths, the veined marble of the grand staircase. The men smoothed down their trousers, creased from the journey; the women had all visited the hairdresser for the occasion. The tickets safe in their wallets were a birthday gift, a wedding present, purchased long ago for a once-in-a-lifetime splurge. Darkness descended on the auditorium, and was greeted by their thrilled whispers: it would sweep away worries, debts, and loneliness. Every evening, when Cléo came on stage, the dusty heat of the projectors took her by surprise, even in the small of her back.

The dancers burst forth, shot through with arching grace, arms open and slightly rounded, they redefined the horizon: a glittering line of identical polished smiles, a set of regimented legs, a swishing and spangled exuberance.

As the spectators left the theater, they passed the dancers without recognizing them: pale, tired girls with lacquer-dulled hair.

Cléo had read this: the fascination of babies with the sheen of a porcelain plate came from our ancestral fear of dying of thirst.

Cléo had read this: the invention of the sequin was accidental. It was down to Henry Rushman, an employee of a company in New Jersey that disposed of plastic waste by crushing it. So many years spent putting up with the din of the machines until that day in 1934, when, just as Rushman was about to leave the workshop, he'd noticed in the vat, among the debris, a minuscule gem with a glint of turquoise. Barely lit in the fading daylight, the crusher was sprinkled with silver and gold, like glittering mica. The residue was reflecting the light.

Sequins emerged from what was deemed worthless; theirs was the beauty of uncertainty. Sometimes it was put to Cléo that all this was trashy, just like the diamanté necklaces resting on her solar plexus, those ruby-red rhinestones circling her waist.

It was all fake, and the disturbing beauty of this world depended on that, she would retort. The girls pretended to be naked, they exaggerated their joy on stage for all of ninety minutes, and sang "*Ça c'est Paris!*" when they hailed from Ukraine, Spain, or Clermont-Ferrand. Sweat stained the satin of their bustiers, its yellowish trace lingering despite dry-cleaning; G-strings were doused in antibacterial spray; fishnets dug into the soft part of the thighs, leaving criss-crossing marks. From a distance, no one noticed a thing.

A lighting engineer had taught Cléo that the cheapest panne velvet shimmered under the spotlights, while, conversely, the same lights dulled the sheen of genuine silk. Light conjured away rips, creases, signs of cellulite, scars; it softened wrinkles and the garish red of cheap hair dye. Bustiers made of sequined fabric left scarlet blotches on Cléo's sides, claret nicks under her armpits: bits of plastic sharpened by sweat. From a distance, no one noticed a thing.

D ancing was about learning to dissociate. Feet like daggers, wrists like ribbons. Power and languor. Smiling despite persistent pain, smiling despite the nausea, a side-effect of the anti-inflammatories.

When Cleo was twelve years, five months and one week old, her parents had suggested that she take dance lessons, concerned about her lounging in front of the TV on Wednesdays and Saturday afternoons. Madame Nicolle's classes were packed with pupils from the private Providence School, all those Domitillas, Eugénies, and Béatrices. In the changing rooms, Cléo would hear them mention a weekend in Normandy, vacations in the Balearics, a language course in the States. Mommy's car, Daddy's car. The cleaning lady, the nanny. The season ticket for the Comédie-Française and the Théâtre des Champs-Élysées.

Cléo was careful not to mention her address—a high-rise housing complex in Fontenay—her parents' Ford Escort, and her mother's job: sales assistant in a plus-size clothing store.

The Domitillas' mothers regularly watched the classes, seated on the wooden chairs set up at the back of the hall. They crossed their ankles, but not their knees. All of them flocked around Madame Nicolle, flattering her, and demanding that she be stricter with their daughters. Their fierce desire to lead them towards a future that they themselves had been denied was palpable, that desire to possess daughters who were limpid, ethereal, sylphlike creatures, with bodies cleansed of their bad blood.

All year, Cléo had applied herself to speaking the language of classical ballet, much as one attempts to "pick up the accent" of a foreign language without ever savoring the words. She had tried to acquire the refinement and haughtiness of those Madame Nicolle cited as paragons of "class": princesses, duchesses. Without success.

At the end of the year, Madame Nicolle had suggested to her that she do something else: gymnastics, perhaps? Cléo wasn't lacking in energy. But as for grace . . .

Cléo had returned to the dreariness of Saturdays in front of the TV. And that's where she had seen them for the first time, those dazzling dancers undulating like swift rivers. They introduced the opening titles of her mother's favorite program: *Champs-Élysées*.

Before the presenter, Michel Drucker, dismissed them—*A big round of applause for the dancers as they leave the set*—Cléo drew closer to the small screen to puzzle out their pirouettes, those bursts of joy that they ended with a leap, so far from the affectation of the Domitillas at Madame Nicolle's: this was what she wanted to do.

From the very first modern-jazz lesson at Fontenay's youth and culture center, Stan had shaken her, swept her away, inspired her. He talked hips. Pelvis. Lower abdomen. Solar plexus. Strength. In sweatpants and a black tank top revealing the top of his pecs, he applauded his pupils whenever they mastered a sequence of steps.

Within ten minutes, the bay window of the hall was covered in condensation, the walls dotted with tiny beads of sweat, and the bass of the Grandmaster Flash or Irene Cara remixes was being distorted by the speakers.

The girl that Cléo caught sight of in the mirror, after a diagonal of chassés, step touch, spin, looked nothing like a duchess, with her bangs plastered to her forehead and her crimson cheeks. The girl that Cléo caught sight of in the mirror had acquired, in a few weeks, an invitingly arched back, far from the rigidity of Madame Nicolle's snooty adolescents holding in their stomachs and clenching their buttocks.

In the evening, in her bedroom, with Walkman headphones clamped to her ears, Cléo would divide the time into counts of eight. Push-ups against the wall, 5-AND-6-AND-7-AND-8. Series of abs, AND-1-AND-2-AND-3-AND-4. Balancing exercise AND-7-AND-8.

Stan's lessons were a blend of worship, celebration, and concentration. AGAIN: Stan demanded that they start again, do it again. The pain of a stitch in her side winded Cléo, but that pain was nothing but a steep path, a slope. Once climbed, all that remained was the glow of deliverance.

Cléo applied herself to copying exactly what Stan was demonstrating, to mastering a movement so it imprinted itself on the fibers of a muscle, which Cléo pictured as a steak streaked with coral blood. It was then, when the body complained, implored, that it had to be imposed upon.

Cléo knew things that thirteen-year-old girls don't. Obeying without questioning. Applauding Stan at the end of class even if he'd told her off for a full hour and a half. Thanking him for it, even. Starting again. In the evening, being unable to sleep because her legs wouldn't stop shaking under the sheets. Upon waking, feeling the stiffness of brutally stretched calves; after her shower, rubbing camphor into taut hamstrings. Her parents mocked her limping like an old lady in the morning. Never a day without some new pain, somewhere or other.

Stan had specified what must be avoided from now on: Cléo would give up skiing, roller skating, running, and racing down the stairs at full speed. In the evening, while her mother ironed in the kitchen after supper, Cléo would describe this daily military routine she so delighted in: she'd managed to do two spins, and Stan had promoted her from the back row to the one ahead. Stan had gotten annoyed at having to re-explain the sequence to her, but he'd said that *if she became a pro* . . .

The magic words: *if she became a pro*. Ever since they'd been pronounced, Cléo was bursting with impatience. At the table, she tapped her feet. Drummed her index finger. Repeated questions the moment they weren't immediately answered. It felt to her like time was standing still, frozen within these familiar settings: the schoolyard, the cafeteria, the little hut where pupils bought crêpes after school, the Fontenay swimming pool on Saturdays, shopping at Leclerc with her mother, the chore of washing-up for five francs, Saturdays watching the Michel Drucker show, with supper balanced on knees. And, on Sunday evenings, between sadness and relief that Monday meant the end of family confinement, washing her hair, drying it, hearing her parents' annoyed bandying of figures: the maintenance charges had gone up again.

She was in eighth grade. She'd have to wait for middle school to be over, and then high school, like sitting through some interminable speech. The passage of time kept misfiring; it was a wheezing motor that only got going when fueled with sweat and the snapping of fingers in Stan's classes. Dance would fill up her life, there would be nothing else, Cléo had written, fervently, in her diary.

But it wasn't true. She hadn't been able to wait: she'd taken the first fork in the road. Cathy had half-opened the future, and Cléo had rushed forward, one foot in the door, nose in the air, ready to leap over all the squares on the board. Of course Cathy's appearance in Cléo's life was a dream come true.

H er name was Catherine, but she preferred to be called Cathy.

She'd watched Stan's classes from the hall, like those mothers who came to collect their daughters, but Cathy wasn't there to collect her daughter. She'd approached Cléo as, disheveled and sweaty, she was heading to the changing rooms. Hello, could she spare her a few minutes? No one had ever asked Cléo if she could spare a few minutes. Straight pale jeans over camel-colored boots, and camel, too, the long coat; a single peachy shade from lips to cheeks; wide silver hoop earrings; and a flight-attendant's smile. Her name was Cléo? Had she seen the movie *Cléo de 5 à 7*? No? She had to see it, an absolute must!

Cathy was there representing a foundation. Did Cléo have some idea what that meant?

(*Smile.*) Well, the Galatea Foundation supported adolescents who showed ability, had exceptional plans. Cléo, conscious of her sweaty bangs and her burning cheeks, was dancing from one foot to the other.

How lucky she was to have such long hair—Cathy was indicating Cléo's ponytail—she could never wait for hers to grow, no patience (*pout—sigh—mahogany lock twirled around index finger.*)

In short: the foundation awarded educational grants. In all fields.

Stan had closed the door to the dance hall: *Good work, Cléo.*

He was right! Cathy had immediately *spotted* Cléo among the others. That was her job: sniffing out talent (*index finger placed on tip of nose.*)

More beautiful than a mother and more fascinating than a friend, Cathy hummed a refrain that adults didn't hear, she was fluent in an adolescent language sprinkled with magical words: *future, spotted, exceptional.*

Pretty Anne Keller, who played opposite Sophie Marceau in *La Boum 2*? It was Cathy who'd *spotted* her in a dance class, made her do a *test*. The foundation had done the rest. Bingo. Veronika, on the cover of the latest issue of *20 Ans*? Ditto. It was Cathy who'd presented her to the photographer David Hamilton. And she had nothing like Cléo's charisma.

Cléo had shrugged her shoulders, disappointed: she didn't want to become either a model or an actress.

Of course! Cathy had mentioned those two, but she could name dancers, sportswomen, and budding stylists . . . As long as they were aiming at excellence!

Surely Cléo wasn't going to stay at this youth and culture center for years? One had to show ambition when one had the abilities. If Cléo was interested, Cathy could come back to talk to her about it? Meet up on Saturday? Here?

SPOTTING, SPOTTED, TO SPOT, *transitive verb*: to see, recognize, notice someone or something among others.

C léo had bounded up to the supper table, there was something she must tell them; her mother shushed her with a wave, maybe when the TV news was over.

In Paris, the prostitutes of the Rue Saint-Denis were demonstrating against their scheduled eviction. In Nantes, Catholic traditionalists threatening to burn down a cinema showing the latest Godard, *Je Vous Salue Marie*, had been greeted by punks armed with buckets of water, stink bombs, and firecrackers.

The actress being interviewed, Myriem Roussel, was raving about her good fortune: Jean-Luc Godard had *spotted* her in a dance class.

Cléo had had to hang on until the weather forecast to tell her parents that: a smart woman / a foundation / a grant / amazing schools / learn lots / my future.

They're looking for ugly girls? her little brother had asked, sniggering. No, she replied, haughtily: for girls with exceptional plans.

Saying these words projected her beyond the rectangle of the dining room, beyond their shriveled existence. Far from her parents slumped on the sofa, backs broken from putting up with everything. It was awful, their sluggish life, lost in pointless bitterness, like in a maze, slamming the weather forecast for saying any old thing, the sales for never being true sales. Her parents' mission seemed to be rooting out rip-offs—

they were triumphant whenever they had proof of some error on a receipt.

If applying for her grant had to be paid for, it was out of the question. You hear about that kind of con all over the place. No thank you.

Her mother's eyelashes stood up, short little sticks stiffened with mascara that, by evening, flaked over her cheeks; Cathy's long eyelashes curled up, gracefully.

Cléo had returned to her room with relief, extricating herself from their banality as though from a neighborhood in which she'd lost her way for years.

Everything was in place for the rest of the *story*. The future looked intoxicating.

T hat Saturday, Cathy was there, as promised, behind the bay window, giving her a little wave. She had suggested a Coke in the cafeteria.

She listened to her talking, solemnly nodding her head, like in those American TV series. Oh, the joy of being questioned. *Tell me about yourself.* Did Cléo already know which high school she'd go to? Was she a cinephile? It was important, for an artist, to take an interest in other art forms. Painting? What was she reading? Did she have friends, or did she prefer to confide in her mother? No best friend? That hardly surprised Cathy: the moment one wasn't like everyone else . . . Most teens seemed so frightfully conventional; she, too, had felt lonely at school. But maybe that was the price one had to pay when destined for better things.

Talking of which, had Cléo drawn up a list of the training courses she might like to attend?

Oh, the joy of saying those names, read in *Danser* magazine: the summer course in Montpellier, and the one at the Centre de Danse International Rosella Hightower, in Cannes.

Fine, but Cléo surely wasn't afraid of leaving France? She must think bigger! Ambition always impressed juries: why not audition for the High School of Performing Arts, in New York, this summer? The school in *Fame*! Cléo had seen the movie, of course?

Well, it's just that . . . it hadn't been on TV, and she only occasionally went to the movies, and English wasn't her strong point . . . And anyway, her parents would never let her go so far away on her own. Not before she was fifteen. Or even sixteen.

Perfect! They just had to add to the file that Cléo needed to take English lessons. And she mustn't worry: Cathy was an expert when it came to parents (*wink*). She'd talk to them. It was only normal for parents to worry, but if one loved one's children, one didn't stand in the way of their desires. She had a son herself. He was almost Cléo's age, and lived with his grandmother in the Drôme. A complicated story, she missed him a lot . . . Cathy had gone quiet. (*Staring into space. Silence.*) Cathy's son, a reassuring marker: a charmingly sad mother was familiar territory.

And . . . was it complicated to fill in, this Galatea form?

Cathy had ruffled her bangs: no worries, she'd take care of everything.

She'd have to be patient. And not get too carried away, because the foundation had its criteria . . . Cathy wasn't on the jury, she just presented the applications. But she didn't deny herself pushing some more than others. (*Smile. Wink.*)

That evening, Cléo had looked in the dictionary for the definitions of: *cinephile / validity / criteria*.

When she closed her eyes, the Galatea Foundation appeared to her in the form of an old building, a kind of cream-colored clinic, with a garden enclosed by high cast-iron railings, and corridors paced by sleek-haired women laden with files that they submitted to men in suits: *exceptional plans*.

Cléo's CinemaScope reverie was laden with concerns: New York? She wouldn't even know how to ask for directions there. And where would she sleep? She wouldn't know anyone. Would have even fewer friends than here. She was dozing off, ashamed of herself, of her cowardice that was just like her parents', of her lack of ambition, which Cathy hadn't yet flushed out.

On Friday evening, her mother had answered the phone. Her mother who was now cooing. Delighted! Cléo has told us so much about you. Wonderful! What good news! Thank you so much.

Her mother rejuvenated, buoyant, to Cléo: you've passed the first selection!

C athy had arranged to meet her on Wednesday, at 5 P.M.; this initial success must be celebrated.

Cléo had never been to this brasserie, close to the Place de la Mairie. With its burgundy banquettes, dark-waistcoated waiters, and muted music, it seemed to Cléo that wherever Cathy went, even here, in Fontenay, she ended up in refined surroundings. Cléo just couldn't picture her unloading a dishwasher, or cursing a skewed rug, like her mother.

She'd given her a lift home. Once she'd turned the ignition off, she'd leaned back against the window, let me take a look at you.

(*Frown. Bottom lip bitten.*) Clothes were important. Especially for an artist. They said who one was. And Cléo was no longer a child. She had more *creativity* in her than her outfit suggested. When one had a lovely figure, one shouldn't hide it.

With seatbelt between breasts and cheeks burning, Cléo was conscious of how ordinary her clothes were: this striped acrylic sweater, these dull cotton trousers chosen by her mother, her fake-leather bomber jacket, a gift from her grandmother at Christmas, when some of her classmates wore real Chevignon ones.

So, why not go on a girls' shopping trip to Paris on Saturday afternoon? They'd take the time to find her a style. It would be *mega fun*! Roles reversed, Cathy, clasping her hands, playful, imploring, adolescent.

What's your favorite district? Cathy had asked. Cléo had mentioned the Créteil Soleil shopping mall, and also the Forum des Halles, she'd been there with her cousin.

Cléo's Paris was the city of Christmas shopping and summer sales. And the city you visited accompanied by teachers, Beaubourg in the sixth grade, and the Tour Saint-Jacques in the seventh. A distant city, but within the suburban RER A's reach, four stations from Fontenay's damp and draughty platform. The carriages, with their graffiti-scrawled seats, smelt of moist cigarettes, and men would sit opposite her and her mother, legs splayed, eyes roving from one to the other and, lately, lingering on Cléo. A blaring city you came home from exhausted, ears ringing with the overexcited voices of the NRJ radio presenters, as broadcast in the Forum's stores, and dazed from the deft zigzagging of pedestrians, avoiding each other without slowing down.

Her mother had given her fifty francs: no way was she being kept by anyone. That Cathy shouldn't go around imagining that Cléo was a pauper.

Cathy's Paris knew nothing of the bustle at the Forum des Halles; it was all winding lanes with narrow pavements, in which sleepy antiquarians kept an eye on piles of gilded treasure. They seemed to be charmed by Cathy, and her chirrupy laughter, when she confessed to "expensive tastes, a love of the fabulous."

Cathy, in a black dress and short leather jacket, took her arm to cross the road, like a friend in a movie. In an American bookshop, she bought her a thick magazine called *Dancing*, without asking the price. In a perfume store on the Champs-Élysées, saleswomen in royal-blue suits had called Cléo *mademoiselle*: Cléo, being sprayed with distilled mists, pink florals and bergamot, sweet rains, and mellow musk; Cléo, being sniffed by fairies bending over her, determined to find her the identity of an aroma. Cathy in the fitting room at the Galeries Lafayette: she must try on this skirt—with a lovely figure, one could get away with anything. Cléo and Cathy at the cash register, Cléo embarrassed, her mother had given her fifty francs and . . .

Cathy cutting her short: she certainly wasn't going to talk money at her age! Cléo tried to retain all of it: the booksellers along the embankment; the pinkish nose of the puppy in the pet store on the Quai de la Mégisserie, the whiff of straw and urine; the salesgirls' legs sheathed in the sheerest pantyhose, their feet pinched into patent pumps; the forceful rush of a mauve and brown Seine, and the hazy wall of fog rising around a horizon of stone: the bridges.

At the tearoom, Cathy had chosen for her. The waitress had taken Cléo to be her daughter; Cléo had been bowled over by that, that a stranger could find a hint of Cathy's smile in her.

Was love anything like this gushing feeling, this great nonsense of giddiness and smiles, this desire to put the present on pause?

T he following Wednesday, Cathy, in the hall, deep in conversation with a blond girl in a sky-blue leotard and matching short skirt, whose hair was in a tight bun. Cathy had given a vague wave, distractedly, while still talking. When Cléo had emerged from the changing rooms, Cathy wasn't there anymore.

Ousted replaced forgotten.

But she had returned that Saturday, all musk and spice, her mahogany hair sleeker than ever. Had applauded Cléo the moment she came through the door from the class: she stood out from everyone else! Had her parents come to see her dance recently? No? Shame!

Cathy wasn't supposed to talk about it, but she'd encountered a member of the foundation who was surprised Cléo's file still hadn't been completed. That boded very well. All that was missing was a pretty photo. Cathy would take care of that, a mere formality. And she must meet her parents, now that things had gotten moving. Saturday?

Her mother had arrived late at the youth and culture center. She didn't hear Stan exclaiming, YES CLÉO!

Cléo whom Cathy applauded as she passed the glass door, whom her mother kissed half-heartedly, her daughter with the sweat-soaked leotard and burning cheeks.

Her mother had grilled Cathy with persnickety questions: if, by any chance, her daughter got the grant and went off to

Cannes, or wherever, who would be with her? It's not that she had *that* sort of mind, but still . . . Should they open a special bank account in Cléo's name, despite her age? And as for the photos, they wouldn't be advancing the fee.

Her mother's voice pricked, and pricked again, like a shrill sewing machine.

Cathy, soft as silk, to her mother: you must be very proud of your daughter.

Her mother had paused before agreeing, as if she'd just been given a tricky puzzle to solve.

Well, she sure dresses well, your Cathy; her coat, it's no knock-off, her mother had said in the car. Must pay well, her foundation.

Customers were scarce at the store for "comfortable, classic, and well-made" clothes; her mother complained that, now, women only went for jeans that flattened their bottoms, or sweatpants that were about as flattering as pajamas. Cathy, at least, had classic and impeccable style.

Her parents had signed the consent slip: I, the undersigned, confirm that I consent to Cléo, my daughter, attending a photo session to complete her file for the Galatea grant.

Much as Cléo had protested that such mistrust was "mortifying," her father had added the following, by hand: owing to Cléo's age, the photos must be submitted to him before being released.

So many new things in Cléo's life. Smells: those pervading Cathy's car, the sweet heliotropes of her perfume, Opium, mixed with the russet whiff of leather. Fabrics: the crimson silk of a scarf Cathy had untied from around her neck to hand to Cléo on a day she'd forgotten her own.

Cléo's denim skirt, scarf, and turquoise mohair sweater had suddenly, in a single morning, made her the center of attention in her class. Gone was the boring, flat-chested, no-eyeliner Cléo, interested in nothing but her dancing, who didn't smoke or drink, who'd never been nabbed at the Auchan mall, who had no boy in her sights.

Cléo had told them all about the foundation, relishing the wide-eyed reactions and questions. The following day, a trio of eighth graders had called her over during recess: was she Cléo? How much was the grant? Did it work for sports, too?

Cléo who was now greeted by the less impressionable, too, ninth graders whose high heels rang out in the corridors. They scribbled boys' names in the margins of their notebooks during the lessons they deigned to attend; the teachers sighed as they called their names for the register, absent again; they squinted as they lit their cigarettes.

A few skeptics pursed their lips: Cléo would end up stark naked in a magazine, it happened every day. Nonsense, another girl would protest. Cathy was a woman! Not some old pervert!

They repeated, like they'd met her, this name with its familiar contours, from the long coat to the mahogany locks: Cathy. Cléo touched by a miracle, the bearer of a *story* whose next chapter they waited to hear every morning, fussing around her as if for a wedding, or a baptism. *Any news from Cathy?*

At breakfast, her mother had inspected her, from her high ponytail down to the sneakers Cléo had picked for the photo session: perfect. The quiet street Cathy had parked in belonged to a Paris of elderly figures in beige overcoats. The building was as fancy as a museum, those balconies, those colonnades, that marble entrance hall with its parquet floor covered in forest-green carpet. The narrow elevator lurched to a halt, Cathy had jumped, like a kid: everything in this neighborhood had a whiff of the old!

The shutters in the apartment were closed, the curtains drawn. A round table, a few chairs, a rolled-up carpet, as if for a removal. Cathy had emptied an ashtray, cursing, *they* could have at least cleaned the place.

She'd been patient, reassuring Cléo when she declared herself "mega ugly" on the Polaroids Cathy showed her as the shoot progressed. She just needed to *relax*.

TO RELAX: to become less tense or anxious, to free one's mind of preoccupations, of nervous or intellectual tension, to loosen up, to be without conflict or aggression.

The hundred-franc note had surprised and embarrassed Cléo: they didn't know if she'd be selected, and her parents didn't want any debts . . .

It was in no way an advance on the grant, just fair compensation for her time, Cathy had explained. And one didn't say "paid," but rather "remunerated."

But this—Cathy had pulled an emerald-green leotard out of a pink plastic bag—was a gift.

Her father had whistled like a young man when Cléo had pulled the banknote out of her pocket, his little girl was a star! He'd looked at the Polaroids Cathy gave them for a long time: that was definitely his Cléo, very natural. They could give one to her grandmother.

Cléo had insisted on having supper in her leotard, her mother had inspected the seams on it, impressed: Repetto was a whole different thing to Carrefour. But you had to be able to afford it.

C athy had called two days later, to invite Cléo for a meal in a restaurant, to *discuss* things; Cléo's father had been concerned: let's hope it's not to break bad news.

Cléo seated opposite Cathy in this Parisian establishment, its walls hung with portraits of regulars: Alain Delon, Christie Brinkley, Brooke Shields. Cléo, thirteen years, four months, and eleven days old, who, with her finger, points out to Cathy an anchorwoman at the neighboring table, instantly rebuked with *we don't do that*. Cléo who agrees, despite not really knowing what Cathy's on about, when she proclaims that an artist must be *open. Not uptight*.

If Cléo's file is accepted, she'll need to show proof of *maturity* in front of the judges. Show them what she's made of.

Cléo who agrees, despite not really knowing what Cathy's on about, except that this speech confirms a boundary line between her and her parents. And what luck to be on the right side, the beautiful side of the line. Cléo who, on this day, is smitten with the décor of her new life: the heavy, immaculate tablecloth, stiff as countryside bedsheets, the attentiveness of the waiter, Cathy's manners, which she copies exactly: the little fork for the slice of smoked salmon, the lips one dabs with the scarlet-edged napkin. The appreciative looks of two men, there to greet Cathy, that linger on her—Cathy's always in such lovely company.

Cléo sitting cross-legged on her bed, that evening, who, in her diary, vows to be "up to it." Why her, 1m 68cm, brown hair with hazel eyes? And why not her?

O ne of the most influential members of the jury had read her file and wished to meet her! Cathy promised Cléo's mother that she'd stay with her during the interview.

The man who opened the door of the apartment seemed older than her father; Marc talked to her with the concerned tone of a headmaster: many young girls got carried away as soon as they passed the initial selection. But whereas Cathy spotted potential, his task was to make sure the girls' plans had that little something extra.

What did she think she had, that was special?

Her leaps. Her fan kicks! And . . . she never got tired. The six hours of dancing a day for the New York course didn't scare her.

Her file was promising. But it lacked a bit of *pep*, it was a bit *staid*.

Cathy leaning towards her, gentle: you understand? *Staid, that means sensible.*

A bit too sensible, stressed Marc.

Cléo's heart where her stomach should be, her stomach up near her throat, her heart wide as a blackish puddle to be swallowed, gone the knowing looks, the attentiveness, and Paris.

That's what they were here for, Cathy reassured her. They were a team, together they'd find that little something that would set her apart from the rest.

Cléo was furious to hear herself quavering in a baby voice, sounding defeated, as she said there was nothing special about her, absolutely nothing: her mother had even mistaken another newborn for her, at the maternity clinic. Lucky that she had this thing, a birthmark, she said, indicating her thigh through her trousers.

Amusing, that. Right, Cléo, *dare to show it, or are you chicken?*

On hearing that dated expression, Cléo had almost burst out laughing, but instead just unbuttoned her trousers, and pointed at the brown mark at the edge of her panties.

Cathy had nodded, Cléo could get dressed now, and thanked her, it was time to go.

In the car, she'd handed her a hundred-franc note, and a cube tied with ribbon, it would bring her luck when facing the judges, soon: Opium by Yves Saint Laurent. Her perfume. They would share the same smell. (*Wink.*)

What was worth hundred francs? Mentioning her birthmark? Lowering her trousers? She hadn't even danced!

Daring, Cathy had replied. Not letting yourself get flustered. Knowing how to improvise was essential for a dancer. The judges would do their best to destabilize her. It was up to keen candidates to stay cool. Just like on stage.

Her father's pride when Cléo had told him that all had gone well, without elaborating any further. There was a thrill to hiding the beginnings of a parallel existence, these adults focusing on her future. Cléo's secret felt intoxicating. She was triumphing over her parents with the utmost tact. The apartment would be a secret little island, Cathy had said, Cléo could come into her own there, become who she dreamed of being.

Before falling asleep, Cléo had inhaled little sniffs of Opium, a cloud of sweet smoke.

Danger had the warm breath of a dozing animal.

Those gifts Cathy gave her every time she came to the youth and culture center. To celebrate the end of winter. For that successful triple spin. For getting 15/20 in French. For nothing. Because.

A coconut-flavored lip gloss, a *Flashdance* poster, a diary you could lock with a miniature key—another little *island*. A small blue box stamped Christian Dior: a palette of eye shadows. The silky powder under the pad of her index finger, lustrous bronze, marron glacé, khaki green. Cléo had mumbled that she couldn't wear it either at school or at home. But in her company, she could, Cathy had objected. She could do everything.

The following morning, during recess, Cléo, thirteen years, five months and two days old, had perched coolly on the low wall in the schoolyard, as the cold and condensation muffled the words she was spouting as fast as a runaway ball: she'd blown him away, that old Marc, she'd managed to *improvise*, the grant, it was in the bag. Huddled around her, some of them wrinkled their noses: what "exceptional" ability had she demonstrated? Cléo, with a weary expression, explained again: it was a question of *maturity*. Her classmates passed the bottle of Opium around, under the schoolyard awning, safe from the supervisors. Carefully, they half-opened the Dior palette: how lovely it was. And mega expensive. You could only find them at the Printemps Nation store. Aline, from the ninth grade, sneered that no one gave anything for nothing. A bit shady, these presents. Cléo shrugged, Cathy knew tons of people who worked for designer labels, and who said anything about "nothing"? Building up a solid file was a real slog.

Anyhow, who wanted to go to the movies, Sunday afternoon, in Vincennes? Cathy had recommended *L'Année des Méduses* to her, Valérie Kaprisky was mega beautiful!

After the movie, Cléo had treated them all to hot chocolate; the waiter had recounted the coins left as a tip: five francs, hadn't she made a mistake?

At the florist, Cléo had picked out the most expensive orchid, and had given it to her mother. The hundred-franc note, that crumpled rectangle, opened up a world of new friendships. Cléo treated everyone to ice creams and waffles, gifted nail polishes, the latest edition of *Première* magazine, and who wanted a fluorescent-pink scrunchie? Cléo, the next installment of whose adventures was eagerly awaited. In the schoolyard, they flocked around her—she who would leave for New York after the *baccalauréat*, to go to the school from *Fame*. She for whom Cathy had bought a copy of *Mademoiselle*, an American fashion magazine, to improve her English. She who had been to see a movie prohibited for those under sixteen: *La Femme Publique*, by Zulawski. Cathy had made her up in the car so it would work, mega funny! She who sported a brand-new bomber jacket. She who repeated: Cathy can't *bear* mediocrity. Sophie Marceau might appeal to parents, and to *Paris-Match*, but she was *conventional*, the complete opposite of Brooke Shields.

One Saturday, Cléo had flicked through a book of photos in a bookstore, and had lingered on a picture of the American actress at the age of twelve, naked in a hip bath, her flat chest slick with oil, eyes heavily made up, all sooty lashes and fuchsia lips. Cathy, leaning over her, had murmured: *Sublime*, Brooke broke the *conventions*.

Well, this Cathy sure was a blessing, Cléo's delighted father would say when she told them about some great exhibition, or shut herself away in her room to finish *L'Amant*, by Marguerite Duras, *recommended* by Cathy.

On the fourth Wednesday, Cathy announced to her that her file had passed the third, and final, selection: Cléo would meet the judges the following week, at an "informal" lunch at the apartment. Sadly, she wasn't allowed to be present when one of her *darlings* was being assessed. (*Piqued little pout.*) Marc would pick her up, and take her back, too. Cathy would give her a call in the evening. The fluttering of her heart, spreading down to her stomach, the moment Cathy had laid a cool hand on her cheek: *I have faith in you.* Her fears, her shyness had vanished: she would go on her own, and would convince the judges, so as not to disappoint Cathy. Cléo's love of showing off, chided by her mother with a *Who d'you think you are*, well, the way Cathy looked at her proved to Cléo that she'd just pulled that off by going to the lunch on her own, without a grumble.

Cléo had returned home exhausted, like after an overlong nap or a too-hot bath.

To her parents, pressing her to describe the lunch in detail, she'd repeated Cathy's phrase: it isn't a done deal yet. But there would be a next time. That was a good sign.

Her father had been amused by her mysterious airs; it was as if Cléo had come out of a job interview with a confidentiality clause attached.

An interview that she'd feared she'd blown, twice: on arrival, Marc had pointed out three young girls, barely older than her, sitting on the sofa in the drawing room. Cléo's disappointment had been so great that Marc had rebuked her: surely she didn't imagine that she was the only one competing for the grant?

Cléo, dancer: when she'd introduced herself to the judges, all four of them, a man had asked her if she'd like to visit the Garnier with him one Sunday afternoon. The Garnier? What's that? The guy had silenced the laughter around him and explained it to her. Immediately, like a racing car determined not to leave the track, Cléo had regained control: going to watch classical ballet didn't appeal to her, what she loved was modern jazz dancing. Like in *Flashdance*. Had he seen it?

A blond waitress, slim as a model, was serving and clearing away. Cléo placed tiny mouthfuls of a fancy dessert on her tongue, hardly daring to use the edge of her spoon to crack the cream meringue decorated with pink hearts. She'd managed not to use the wrong cutlery for the fish. She hadn't mopped up the sauce from her plate. The other girls seemed to be concentrating just as hard.

The muffled beauty of the serious conversations around her, the elegance of the waitress, the sugar candy in the tiny jade-green saucer, all this that she was entitled to, and that her mother wasn't. Cléo felt like crying over her mother's lackluster life, felt like taking home to her the little golden box of matches, choked with love for the mother who didn't have the incredible luck she had.

One of the judges had praised the simplicity of her outfit: with a freshness like hers, jeans and a T-shirt, that was perfect; young girls of today had a propensity for vulgarity that he deplored.

He was called Jean-Christophe and was dressed as if for a wedding, in a shirt and dark jacket. When it was time for coffee, he had risen from the table and suggested to her that they "get to know each other" in the drawing room.

Like Cathy, he asked for her views, her opinions. He leaned over her to recite her a poem, whispered in her ear, sent a shiver down Cléo's spine.

He had heard a good deal about her. Cathy was a fan! Now he understood why. He would be happy to participate, one way or another, in her fine future. Does that mean I've got the grant? she'd asked. Jean-Christophe had smiled, that was jumping the gun a little . . .

Already! she'd exclaimed, when Marc had indicated his watch to her. But she hadn't done anything! She hadn't been asked a single question about her plan! And when she'd brought her dance stuff, in her bag, just in case . . .

Next time, the man had promised. May I? he had asked. Cléo had nodded. The man's lips on her cheek, his light, rapid breathing in her neck: that vanilla aroma made one feel like devouring her. Did she fancy being devoured? Next time?

She'd put the 100-franc note into the cookie tin she kept postcards in. Cléo imagined herself handing it to her parents, and so putting an end to her mother's acrimony, her moaning about being the only one doing the accounts, slamming the useless purchases of her father, who snapped back that she wasn't going to dictate his tastes. Worn-out love meant reproaching each other for not counting the same way. Cléo listened to them from her room, sheltered; she was elsewhere, on the brink of something massive.

The following Wednesday, to her parents, who were astonished that she had to meet the judges again, and to the girls at school, Cléo had trotted this out: given how much the grant was worth, it made sense for the judges to be thorough. The lunches were a *modern* way of assessing the candidates. Everything counted. Especially *maturity*.

When Cléo had mentioned this second ordeal to Cathy, on the phone, she'd been delighted: she'd heard that Cléo had *seduced* a judge, she'd smashed the competition, Cléo's future was in her own hands.

Cléo hadn't seen her the previous time, the twentysomething redhead in a tight blouse who greeted her that day, and then put her army-surplus bag in a closet. Paula was Cathy's indispensable assistant, Marc explained. Cléo watched as the girl bustled about, went to the kitchen, showed everyone their places at the table. Was she a student, an actress, a sportswoman, had she received the grant? Did Cathy take her to the movies, too? Had she given her a bottle of her perfume?

Cléo was ready. Today she would rise above the anonymity of being "almost selected"; she, too, would become indispensable. Like Paula.

Seated beside Jean-Christophe, she chattered away with gusto, imitating a friend—Valérie had called the English teacher a whore in class—and mimicking Stan's American accent: he thought going to "New Yooork" was "a bit prematchurr" for

Cléo. But she didn't give a damn! She'd prove him wrong. Jean-Christophe turned to Marc, what a fighter, this Cléo!

He brought a little fork to the edge of her lips, these oysters were divine; Cléo had politely declined, she didn't like them. Or champagne, too bitter. All the other girls were drinking, Marc had pointed out to her, in his headmasterly tone. Sitting at the other end of the table, they didn't so much as glance at her, engrossed in their conversation with two men not much younger than Jean-Christophe.

Jean-Christophe had skimmed through her file. And . . .

Do you think you're a Galatea girl, Cléo?

Marc, arms crossed, waited for her reply, just like at their first meeting. The other guests didn't seem to notice the anxious hole Cléo was sinking into, dug by the serious tone of the question.

Yes, of course she was a Galatea girl because dancing was her whole life, everything, she'd work twice as hard, and the same went for English—in fact, since she'd been going to see undubbed movies, it was improving.

The others also work hard; tell me why I should choose you rather than her, over there?

He indicated an apple-cheeked girl sitting at the table, beside another judge.

Was Cléo more . . . modern? More daring? Less . . . conventional? She, who was an artist?

She nodded, yes. Yes yes.

Cléo was lucky, he adored dancers. Preferred them to musicians. They were so relaxed. At ease. Like her, his *adorable little fiancée*. Cléo burst out laughing, she was too young to have a fiancé.

Friend-fiancé, perhaps? To begin with?

Did Cléo have a boyfriend of her own age? With whom she . . . No? Cléo wasn't *frigid*, at least?

The word "frigid" sunk, like some misshapen lead weight, in the pit of Cléo's stomach.

At least Cléo hadn't let herself be *fiddled with* by some kid who didn't know what he was doing.

All the blood in Cléo's body on hold, listening out.

Might we consider the apartment like a little island of pleasure? A world apart? Far from all banality? Far from all conventions, all judgments about age? Do you permit me that, Cléo?

May I?

All these question marks, no one had ever asked for her permission to do anything at all, this gentleness, this amazing respect from Jean-Christophe, Cléo adored it, his words reduced to a whisper. But Jean-Christophe's tongue was like an oyster in her mouth, dead and alive, wet and slimy, moving too much and too far, the smell of wine combined with the spices in that sauce at lunch, breath that was bitter and stale, his tongue like some rubbery instrument searching, probing. An irrepressible urge had seized her, to rid her mouth of any residue of saliva, of flesh. Cléo had wiped her mouth with the back of her hand.

Well, that's not very nice, Cléo!

Was Cléo tense? Dancers were at ease with their bodies, normally. Jean-Christophe astonished. Offended? Disappointed?

If necessary, Paula could give her a relaxing massage, he suggested. She was brilliant at it.

May I?
Close your eyes, Cléo.

Cléo, thirteen years, five months, and however many days, had consented. To say no was to be *frigid*.

Behind Cléo's closed eyes, galaxies of coppery shapes streaming past, and the cacophony of her blood throbbing in her temples, all the commotion of an undertow. Orange cotton dress pushed up, tights pulled down, legs limp, tangled. Careful not to open her eyes. Doing her best. Because this was just a way of testing her, of being sure she didn't get flustered. The metal of a cold ring, the warm, tense fingers, the wet breath.

You must relax, Cléo . . .
Come on. Relax
Relax, dammit

The fingers like annoyed insects, exasperated at not managing to go where they were determined to go anyhow, nocturnal insects that would quit once the light was back on, you just had to keep perfectly still.
Not very sexy. Stiff as a board, Cléo.
Sorry, but she had to go to the bathroom. Barefoot on the tiled floor, lost in this apartment, of which she'd only ever seen the dining room, she pushed open first one door, then another. Sitting on the toilet seat, her breathing jerky, Cléo counted the small blue and beige tiles on the floor. 5-6-7-AND-8. *Little fiancée.* Was that good or bad? Already a voice was calling her, CLÉOOO.

Jean-Christophe was patting the sofa with his palm for her to return to her place. And so Cléo's words had adapted to this downward twist in the *story*, had improvised: she'd just noticed, she had her period it was the first time really bad stomach pain so sorry.
Some other time.

C léo walked, and the streets crisscrossed like some impenetrable web, Rue de l'Assomption, Avenue Kléber, Avenue de Wagram. The Seine seemed heavier and more velvety than at Nogent, where her parents loved to stroll in the spring. Cléo had stopped one passerby, and then a second, how did one get to Fontenay? Neither knew Fontenay.

She'd gotten on to the No. 30 bus without thinking, it would transport her further away from the apartment. Cléo closed her eyes, lulled by the warmth of the heating at her feet, the purring of the motor during traffic jams. The driver had told her where to get off to pick up the RER, had given her a half-fare ticket, must have thought she was under thirteen.

Behind her closed eyes, the shapes had reappeared, a flashing of random images, like the slides her father would spread across the coffee table after vacations. The insects. The fingers. The dancers. Her uncle, who, every New Year's Eve, kept checking his watch so as not to miss the TV broadcast of the Lido show. He'd worked there as a waiter. Cléo knew the anecdote by heart: once the show was over, the dancers would slip away through a discreet door, and a taxi would await them outside to whisk them away from the liberties taken by spectators convinced they had a right to them. Pleasure for the eyes, her uncle would say, wagging his finger. The dancers were not to be touched.

She'd turned down supper, wanting only a yogurt; her brother brayed that she was on a diet, her father rolled his eyes. All four of them were bound by a tacit contract, that of a family from which a few Wednesdays had extracted her. Cléo couldn't complain to anyone about having been bitten. She belonged to the secret of an apartment she didn't know the address of.

Her head was spinning as if she had been flung from a plane, a cosmic solitude. In the middle of the night, she'd been gripped by waves of nausea, along with spasms and bile. Cléo's teeth were chattering. Her sheets seemed steeped in the smell of the bottle of Opium hidden under her bed, a stench of musk and patchouli. Cléo opened the window wide, the fresh air receded, it cleared away nothing.

She'd have liked to cancel the day ahead until she understood. No classrooms with an audience of girls awaiting her, hungry for new episodes: Cléo and Cathy, Cléo and Galatea, Cléo and the hundred-franc notes. To stay shut away in her bedroom, with its magazines and grubby soft toys stuffed in a suitcase, and, in the bottom drawer, a checked dress from when she was ten, which her mother meant to give to charity but couldn't bear to part with.

Her parents often said, with a sigh, that Cléo saw everything as a tragedy. Maybe they were right. She might have misunderstood what had happened at the lunch, and—for that matter—what had happened?

Cathy's cheery voice on the phone, two days later, had filled Cléo with relief, tinged with hope. Like at the beginning. But not entirely like at the beginning. Cathy left long silences at the other end of the line; what were they about, these silences that Cléo had covered, apologizing: she'd been out of sorts.

Her heart was rattling between her floating ribs, like that of a punished puppy desperate to be stroked once more. As she'd hung up, she'd felt it, resting, lightly, on her lungs: a water lily, like in that Boris Vian novel she'd read in her French class. Not the symptom of an illness, but quite the reverse, the beginnings of a recovery: all was not lost. Cathy had suggested that they *discuss* things. Cléo would have to show that she was worthy of this second chance.

On the burgundy banquette in the brasserie, Cathy awaited her, luminous, in a sky-blue sweater and white trousers.

These lunches were about testing her *ability to adapt*. Was she going to run away every time *something unconventional* happened? Would she storm out on a capricious teacher in New York?

Cléo was sure of it: Cathy didn't know, about the fingers. Otherwise she'd have mentioned it. Cathy was all about the beautiful. Devoted to the exceptional. What Cathy loathed was *weakness of character*.

Had Cléo shown that weakness at the lunch when she'd allowed moves to be made? Or had she shown it when she hadn't allowed enough moves to be made?

That shame over the fingers against that shame about being *frigid*.

Might it be possible, next time, to sit beside another judge, rather than Jean-Christophe?

Cathy, suspicious: whatever for? He went a bit heavy on the champagne, sure, but he was a competent man. Moreover, he'd been very understanding on the phone, hadn't *closed the door* on Cléo at all. According to him, she needed to think about what she *really* wanted.

Cléo had nodded, *really* wanting the grant, was that wanting the fingers? Not wanting the fingers, what was that proof of?

Cathy had dropped her off outside her home, had held the door wide open for her: an invitation to return to her former world, without a future and without Galatea.

The distraught Cléo of spring 1984 was like a marionette with its strings cut, dislocated; a little dysfunctional heap that her parents showed, like some bafflingly smelly bundle of washing, to various doctors: a gastroenterologist for her vomiting, a dermatologist for a rash of rough, purplish patches, an allergist for nocturnal asthma.

At night, gripping the turquoise blanket, she was convulsed with retching and sobbing, her mother held her hand, her brother snuggled up to her, what's wrong, Cléo?

What was wrong was sorrow heaped upon sorrow, lies multiplied by lies.

One shame concealing another. The shame of letting that be done to her, and the shame of not managing to *relax* enough to let that be done to her.

We won't make a big deal about this, Marc had said, afterwards.

T en days without dancing, even at her age, came at a cost: at the end of the class, Stan had teased her about her red-faced breathlessness. When she re-emerged from the changing room, he'd caught up with her: the lady who sometimes came to see her was waiting for her outside.

She'd hastily offered her cheek to Cathy, knocking her knee on the gearshift, nose buried in the Opium-infused hair, overcome by the tinkling laughter.

For now, Cléo's file was on pause. Cléo needed to gain a little *maturity*. But Cathy had pleaded her cause at the foundation. And they had thought that, perhaps,

If you're interested in this proposal

PROPOSAL: a plan or suggestion put forward for consideration by others. Synonyms: offer, proposition

Before even knowing what why how, Cléo had nodded her head vigorously; a proposal, that was another chapter, not an ending. Yes, she was interested.

But . . . Cléo didn't even know what Cathy was about to say, Cathy exclaimed (*wink*). She'd got her champion back! No dwelling on the past, moving forward! Precisely what Cathy was after for this assistant's job.

Cléo had been gripped by a final, tiny doubt: what if she was no good at it? Would she be excluded from Galatea forever?

Do you trust me, Cléo? Had Cathy ever lied to her? *I can sniff out talent, don't forget.*

A professional of thirteen years, six months, and eight days old, who'd immediately gotten herself organized with the kind of determination associated with New Year's resolutions. She'd be worthy of this work *remunerated* by the Galatea Foundation. Not jealous of the girls she'd select, because her turn would come. Cathy had promised that to her: those awarded grants were between thirteen and fifteen years old. Cathy had been wrong to rush things. Next year, she'd reapply.

Like that first day, the news was announced to her parents with a twirl: learn something new, select files, earn a little money. Her appetite returned with the suddenness of summer rain: so, not sick any more, her brother suspected as much, she'd been faking it!

Well played, her father had said: you've got a foot in the door. Your grant will come. Well played, her mother had said: as long as you don't devote too much time to it.

She'd bought a notebook at Monoprix, one hundred and fifty squared pages. Dividers. Two Stabilo pens.

First names in the left-hand column. In the right-hand one: the plans of each girl. Their dreams. A blue divider for the girls at school, a red one for the pupils at the dance center. Cathy had advised Cléo to favor girls from a modest background. Not the ambitious ones, with dreams of a career. The Galatea Foundation's mission was social.

The first girl to be approached, in the youth-center changing rooms, was an aspiring actress moaning about the fees at the Cours Florent drama school, who'd seemed dubious: never heard of the Galatea Foundation. Cléo had delivered her spiel with conviction. The girl had left her phone number.

Cathy had pouted: seventeen years old? If the girl had potential, she would have been *spotted* already. And also, at that age, boyfriends poked their noses into everything. Men just got in the way. (*Wink.*)

At school, having explained her new role, Cléo had instantly found her power to be even more magnetic than when she'd been the Chosen One. Girls shared their aspirations with her, asked her to assess their "plans." Wanted to know how the selection process worked.

Cléo-Cathy gave an edited version of it, with no mention of Jean-Christophe or of *fingers*. The foundation was straight-up: it *remunerated* you, to make up for the time spent completing your file.

But recruiting for the foundation turned out to be trickier than she'd thought. There were the girls who didn't dare, and those who couldn't care less about the future. Those who had no dreams. Those who were supposed to talk to their parents about it, and then didn't. Those who were studying for exams.

Cathy called: *You're not forgetting me?*

Pass her to me, her mother insisted, with an imperious flourish, only to sound instantly rejuvenated:

Good evening, Cathy! You must come over for supper one evening.

S itting cross-legged on the dark-red carpet in her room, with the phone balanced on her knees and her warm breath against the plastic receiver, Cléo was whispering, a rush of jostling consonants: I need t'know what you've decided 'bout Wednesday. Your plan it looks strong to me it'd be mega if you got the grant. But gotta do several interviews . . .

The ribbon of whispers wound its way through the gloom. The bedside lamp lit up the posters pinned to the wall: brown bangs brushed by false eyelashes, the pointed toe of an arched foot, a bare belly shimmering with glitter, the dancers in *Champs-Élysées* on the cover of the TV listings magazine.

From the corridor, her mother's voice: Cléo, I've got calls to make, five more minutes and you hang up. Cléo's breath against the hollow of her damp palm: my mother's getting annoyed gotta go, do I sign you up?

This conversation, repeated dozens of times.

First names in the left-hand column, phone numbers below.

Slowly, girls were starting to give in. Some from the year above called out to Cléo: hey, we wanna ask you something. They wanted to be actresses, do an internship at Jean Paul Gaultier, record an album, get tennis coaching. Impatient to be judged, graded, chosen.

One girl had heard that some other girl had been selected. Who, to her knowledge, had zero talent. She, too, wanted to meet Cathy. The girl on the verge of tears if Cléo hesitated, resisting saying you piss me off Cléo, because Cléo *was* the foundation, Cléo who'd disappeared, been *devoured*, Cléo-Cathy.

After meeting Cathy, they ran up to Cléo in the schoolyard: they could never thank her enough for having encouraged them to introduce themselves. Cathy was a-maz-ing. They were going shopping with her on Saturday. After the previous week's trip on a *bateau-mouche*, tomorrow it would be the photo shoot to complete their file.

Each one of these episodes, the same. A sweater, perfume, theater tickets, a restaurant.

Cathy, on the phone, every other night, now just a voice, praising Cléo about one girl or another. That other girl, however: no.

Like a hunting dog patiently trained to stop retrieving

inedible quarry, a dog that ends up knowing what it's looking for without knowing how it knows, Cléo-the-eagle-eyed, Cléo-the-evaluator looked out for a sharp hip bone showing under briefs in the dance-class changing rooms. Assessed the silkiness of a cheek. The straightness of teeth. The sheen of blond hair. The way ash-blond eyebrows matched the flecks in eyes.

Older girls from the private Providence School would call out to her: did Cléo not remember them? From Madame Nicolle's classes? They simpered: it wasn't the money that interested them, not remotely. But building up a network for themselves. A grant for excellence was important for later: top universities rated evidence of initiative from secondary school onwards. They knew how to sell themselves, lined up their abilities, the languages they'd mastered. When Cléo gave them an appointment they thought too distant, they mewed, like precious little kittens, indignant at having to wait their turn.

The girls at the Maximilien-Perret vocational school approached the chance of a grant like a job. They didn't hide it: they had no plans at all. But they needed money. Cléo liked them for their cool way of doing deals, whistling to hail a friend, keeping their Walkman headphones clamped to their ears when being spoken to, squeezing their tummies into faded jeans, and throwing their heads back when laughing. Their lives wouldn't wobble over mere *details*. They wouldn't slam the door of the apartment, alarmed by a Jean-Christophe. They'd be "pros" who wouldn't rock the boat, whom Cathy valued.

Now, Cléo only ever crossed her path every Wednesday, at 3 P.M., on Place de la Mairie. Cléo would present the new girl to Cathy, *cooing / future / sniffing out talent*.

Cathy *remunerated* Cléo.

Could they go to Paris soon, just the two of them? she pleaded, ashamed, just as they were parting.

Cléo was leaving her childhood behind seamlessly. The days, slow and opaque, washed over her. She felt moved by her parents, their efforts to maintain their role as parents, to act as though they were keeping up, their questions in the evening, at supper. To which Cléo replied by dividing everything by two: the sums of money she earned, the time she spent earning it, the labyrinth she was living in. She observed their blindness calmly, with the indulgence of a passing stranger. Her mother claimed to "sense" her two children, so no need for long conversations. Her mother was a keen reader of the "psychology" columns in magazines.

On Thursday morning, at the school gates, the Chosen One was showing off a Kenzo scarf that was so BEAUTIFUL. Cléo asked if everything had been all right, the way waiters do in restaurants. Sometimes, she thought she glimpsed an evasive look, a silent language of murkiness and embarrassment.

Her marks at school had sunk below average; those other numbers, the rhythm of Stan's classes, offered her hands to cling onto, AND-5-AND-6-AND-7.

Her parents were amazed at how keen she was to clear the table, tidy her room, play Happy Families with her brother. Cléo found a painful pleasure in doing so, she was playing at being the girl they loved, assuming the appearance of something lost, gone, like those dead stars whose lingering glow is admired: Cléo the child.

Cléo imagined herself telling them everything, but that

"everything," they knew it already. Cléo helped Cathy. There was nothing to reveal. Her parents were delighted with their daughter's newfound maturity. Cléo, that character devoid of reason or logic, who hid banknotes she no longer counted, the youngest in the dance class and oldest of all the schoolgirls, whose days were a patchwork of skillful lies, days stitched and re-stitched so they would hold out.

She'd have to hold on for a year, long enough to grow up, and then, doubtless, she'd have gained the maturity necessary for the lunches, for the *fingers*.

She'd had her first period. Alone in the bathroom. From behind the door, her mother explained to her how to use a tampon. Relax. From behind the door, her mother instructed her to "force" it in a bit, it was dead easy, nothing to make a fuss about, nothing to start crying about like that, over a tampon.

S o you're Galatea?"
She'd confronted Cléo under the schoolyard awning, a tall, wiry girl, in a baggy jacket matching her snow-washed jeans, which showed off her Disney Alice socks.

Cléo had reeled off: yes, she did indeed have a job at the Galatea Foundation . . . only to be interrupted by a sneering "blah blah blah."

Galatea might be a foundation, but it was really the name of a mythological character: the creation of a sculptor named Pygmalion, who was so in love with his statue that he brought her to life. The ballet *Coppélia* was based on that very myth, the girl concluded, completing the humiliation of a stunned Cléo, her ignorance tested by a girl from the year below her, in front of the other pupils.

Betty seemed so sure of herself for her age: twelve and a half. She was in seventh grade, and was the star of Fontenay's youth and culture center, a pupil in the advanced classical ballet class. At school, this status didn't count for much, so she compensated with wisecracks like the one that had just caught out Cléo.

Betty wanted to apply. With a lisp (she'd just started wearing braces and struggled with some letters), she specified the price of pointe shoes, and of private coaching to compete for a place at the conservatoire. Cléo listened to her, waiting for a pause to respond, but the girl with the heavy eyebrows and light eyes had, with a flick of the wrist, gathered her hair into a low bun, leaving a few stray commas around the temples, and then, in an arc extending to the tips of her slender fingers, and with her foot pointing skywards, she had opened herself out before the eyes of the amused supervisors. That was an arabesque. And not this: Betty had demonstrated a stiff leg extension very like the one Cléo prided herself on having achieved.

Some seventh-grade girls carried their childhood like a burden—they were nearly 1m 70cm tall, and bra straps left a mark on their shoulders. Others, however, kept their adolescence at bay, zipping their tracksuit jackets right up to their necks to hide the first signs of breasts, stoical in the spring sunshine, their trousers dotted with Nutella stains. Betty maintained a graceful balance between the two. Pretty and already beautiful. She played dodgeball and wore mascara. She entertained, like a butterfly, and no one dared admit to fearing her mockery, her mimicry. With Betty, everything added to her aura. Her first name? It was American, a star's name. And there were loads of songs with "Betty" in the title, one by Bernard Lavilliers, and another by Ram Jam—her mother loved all that "*Whoa, Black Betty*" stuff.

Her amber skin? That was a gift from her maternal grandmother, born in Belize. A mega beautiful country, all palm trees and Club Med beaches; Betty would go there one day. Her surname? That was her father, half-Albanian. A mega dangerous country. No big deal, she never saw him anyway.

The sort of pupils who spat out "wog" spared her: Betty was labeled "exotic."

Betty snooped around, keen to join cliques that she'd quit as soon as she'd won them over. In the cafeteria, she'd put her tray down, decisively, on the table of older girls, presenting her dessert as a kind of offering. A few eighth-graders, huddled around a Chosen One, shooed her away, and continued with their confab, unaware that the younger girl was still there, listening as they passed on Cléo's phone number.

Cléo, sitting cross-legged on the dark-red carpet in her room, with the phone balanced on her knees and her breath against the plastic receiver: you're too young, Betty, the grant's for those aged thirteen and above.

At the other end of the line, quick as a breath: sorry, Cléo, but if *you* were spotted, with your not-so-awesome level of dancing, for me, the grant's in the bag, they'll make an exception.

From the corridor, her mother's voice: you're still on that phone, Cléo, I've got calls to make, in five minutes you hang up.

A ribbon of whispered words winding through the gloom: hey, Betty, that's my mother, getting annoyed, gotta go, it won't work, drop it. And your mother, she wouldn't approve, anyhow.

Betty's irritation, a flurry of jostling consonants: you screwed it up, so my trying for it bugs you, 'cause I'm gonna get it, your fucking grant. Just come over to my place Wednesday, you'll see if my mother doesn't approve.

On both walls of the apartment's corridor, Betty was pinned up, framed. On the dresser. Behind the glass front of a bookcase. On the TV set. Every knick-knack in this overheated apartment seemed resigned to ceding its place to future photos of Betty.

As a baby with brown curls, in the arms of a young girl with heavily made-up eyes. In a field of poppies at around four, wearing a pink hairband. Betty in a lilac leotard, with a bun, eight maybe, at the center of a group of little girls, a school show. Betty, her smile triumphant, on her first pair of pointe shoes. In a short tutu, hair set with a tiara, lifted by a young adolescent in black tights. Saint Betty, eyes down, hands crossed over chest, crowned by artificial flowers. Betty the Fairy, a flounce of white tulle, her photo snapped a meter from the ground, in a grand jeté. Miss Betty, in black and white, with big spidery eyelashes brushing her cheeks. The congratulations of the jury presented to Mademoiselle Betty Bogdani, silver medal awarded unanimously.

Her mother, whom Cléo had taken for her big sister when she'd opened the door, had taken a bottle of Orangina out of the fridge and arranged slices of cake with pink icing on a plate. For once, Betty had invited a friend round.

And then she'd praised her daughter to Cléo: she was serious and reliable. She'd taken herself to school since she was nine. Did babysitting on the weekend. But all that wasn't enough to pay for the pointe shoes, she went through two pairs a month. Not to mention the private coaching: a hundred and fifty francs an hour. Her daughter was destined for a career: she indicated the tangible proof, plastering the walls, of this future.

Betty was stitching ribbons onto her ballet shoes without joining in, like a child bored by grown-up talk.

Betty's mother was pulling other diplomas out of a drawer, and it was so embarrassing, this adult begging Cléo to make an exception, to show understanding. If she could just give her daughter a chance.

They'd finished the rose-flavored cake, watched a soap on TV, and Betty had wiped down the counter and sink with all the thoroughness of an adult.

Her mother had thanked Cléo, she'd be so grateful if she just gave it some thought, had kissed her, the powder on her cheeks smelling of violets, leaving a flowery taste in Cléo's mouth.

This silent soliloquy reverberated, a staccato of syllables, punctuating Cléo's every hour: not Betty not Betty not twelve years old, at the table at those lunches, not Betty at all.

The kid came to find her at every recess: well?

She phoned her in the evening: well?

And, whining: the other girls all had private coaching on Saturdays, getting into the conservatoire was impossible if you didn't. Well??

On Wednesday, May 16, 1984, at 5 P.M., Cléo was walking towards the Place de la Mairie beside an Anaïs or a Stéphanie when a voice, in the distance, made her stop: Cléo, hey, wait for me wait.

All the ways she could have reacted: pushing Betty away with a pat on the back, making her turn around and go back; gripping Betty by the collar of her denim jacket and urging her to give it a rest, her hand could have grabbed Betty's as one does with a child who's about to cross a busy road, her hand should have rested on the young girl's shoulder, obliging her to remain beside her. A hand that would have been firm, would have stopped, prevented, held back, protected. A hand or a few words. Not you Betty. Go away Betty. Shut up Betty.

But not a word had come out of her mouth. Not the slightest move had been made. Cléo had remained a spectator, she had let things happen.

Cathy was closing the car door, rusty hair, tinny laughter.

Without worrying about Stéphanie or Anaïs, the young girl had planted herself in front of Cathy and had reeled off her medals chronologically, like some war veteran before a President of the Republic. Cathy was enchanted, amused, entertained. Not even thirteen years old? (*Dubious pout.*) She could have a word with the foundation about it, some exceptions were, occasionally, made . . .

That very evening, over the phone, Cléo had found herself being rewarded with a: *Quite a find, your Betty.*

Cléo stammered that she had nothing to do with it, she hadn't introduced Betty to Cathy. Cléo had done nothing. Nothing, that was just it. Cléo, thirteen years and seven months old, was overwhelmed by this monologue, known only to her, that took over as soon as the sounds of everyday life ceased, shutters closed, parents in bed: the carousel clattering with scrap-metal words and no one to stop it, no one to go back to the start of the story and calmly examine the facts, to absolve her, or perhaps condemn her.

B etty—was it the following week?—had come towards her in the schoolyard, clutching a transparent pink plastic bag: Cathy had bought her made-to-measure pointe shoes!

All the episodes to come, the pieces of a jigsaw puzzle so simple to assemble: the perfume store on the Champs-Élysées, the puppies in the pet store, the restaurant with walls hung with portraits of stars, the Polaroids, *daring, not to let oneself get flustered*, the banknotes stashed away in a tin, each episode, until the last one.

A puzzle made of dry wood, so its splinters got everywhere, in the slightest chink of silence, of repose. Cléo was bathing in liquid fear, drowning in it.

The merry-go-round of doctors had started up again in May: in front of them, Cléo spoke without saying anything, without giving anything away, a valiant soldier of Galatea.

At the staff meeting, Cléo's main teacher had suggested she redo that year: her average marks meant she couldn't catch up on the classes missed. Her father had given her a long hug—who cares about grades, nothing to lose one's appetite over. In time, she wouldn't remember any of all that. Promise.

But what would she remember, then?

Her mother had announced to her that she'd had Cathy on the phone: they'd decided *together* that it would be best if she took a break: the foundation would still be there next year.

To those who begged her for a meeting with Cathy, Cléo explained that she no longer had the time, what with dancing and classes to catch up on. She denied having been "fired" from Galatea, denied having dangled before them what she could no longer grant; she had nothing more to tell them about, nothing to dazzle them with.

At recess, she watched them, trying to guess which girl had taken her place helping Cathy.

She looked for Betty, who gave her a little nod without coming any closer.

Cléo trying to detect in each girl any trace of *lunches*, of *fingers*.

In June, Cléo had spotted Betty's mother leaving the principal's office. Betty was moving that autumn to a school that specialized in dance: she'd succeeded in getting into the conservatoire. Betty, whom her mother framed in gold.

In June, Stan had gathered the young dancers together after class: his contract was coming to an end. One day, people would pay to see them on stage. It was their responsibility to ensure that spectators left the theater bowled over. That the performance lifted them out of their everyday lives, even just briefly. They should never forget: they were dancing for all those who would never have that freedom.

Stan had stopped talking, and Cléo's tear-streaked little face had made him smile: HEY CLEYO, he'd held out his hand to help her up, and briefly hugged her: what a baby.

Just before their vacation, her parents had given Cléo sixty francs to go and buy herself a swimsuit at the lovely boutique near the town hall.

Cléo had been gearing up for this for weeks: Cathy was in the café, alone. Doubtless waiting for a Cléo. A Paula.

Cathy, in a cropped, greige leather jacket and light trousers, had asked Cléo if she was feeling better, and would she *permit* her to keep in touch? From time to time? Cléo had, once again, agreed. Cathy had placed a calming palm on Cléo's cheek, *no hard feelings, then*, not a question, but a statement.

2

The sender's address, verylucie@free.fr, is unknown to him, and the cryptic subject of the email, "marking a fond memory / 1987," accompanied by an attached picture, makes him want to consign the message to spam.

And yet Yonasz places his index finger on the attachment, a dull click.

"Fond memory 1987" is at the center of the photo, looking straight at the camera, sitting between a fifteen-year-old Yonasz and his father, both caught holding their breath and smiling. Her hands laid flat on the white tablecloth, "fond memory 1987": a sixteen-year-old Cléo.

■ ■ ■

In autumn 1987, Yonasz was starting tenth grade.

He was dawdling in childhood the way one puts off leaving the house on a Sunday, quite the opposite of the girls who, on the morning of September 5, filed through the blue gate of the Lycée Berlioz, those girls he'd known, for the most part, since primary school.

Forgotten were the baggy sweatshirts, and the greasy bangs they pushed aside with ink-stained fingers: over the summer, they had changed both their demeanor and their eyebrows, plucked into a fine, upward line. And extending to their temples was the eyeliner, where the crimson blusher stopped. Under their T-shirts, the assertive bulge of their breasts clamped by an underwire bra, stretching the fabric down to the solar plexus. Below the T-shirt, tightly knotted above the navel, their tummies were bare.

They were meeting up again, excitedly, after two months of vacation, the swell of their voices ricocheting off the corridor's tiled floor, speaking over each other, eager to moan about their holidays: walking forever in mega boring forests, like, isn't nature just *amazing*, getting too close to the shriveled balls of old hippies on naturist beaches. But it beat spending the summer in a Paris full of ruddy-faced English tourists and perverts whose wives were away on vacation.

Yonasz was heading for the cafeteria when a small group caught his attention: a few pupils crouching around a girl sitting on the floor, who had just tripped on the stairs.

And who was prodding the malleolus of her bare ankle with her index finger and pinching her Achilles tendon, before declaring, with real medical authority: it's not swelling. And who, limping, turned down a girl with a plastic bag full of ice cubes from the infirmary: she didn't need a thing.

Her ponytail bounced to the rhythm of her slight limp, and Yonasz found her appearance underwhelming, that plain T-shirt without a logo, and those little-girl eyelashes without mascara. The dark-red silk scarf tied around her neck seemed to belong to her mother.

When the French teacher read their index cards out loud, surname, first name, parents' profession, Cléo explained that she was older than most of them because she'd redone her eighth grade. She didn't really have any favorite books, she preferred movies, Yonasz hadn't seen any of them: *Marche à l'Ombre*, *A Chorus Line*, and *La Femme Publique*.

Lined up on her desk was a pencil, an eraser, and a pair of

scissors; Yonasz found her childish—they wouldn't be cutting out any paper dolls.

Sandra, whom Yonasz had known since junior high, was holding court under the schoolyard awning. She wore her jeans tucked into white cowboy boots and slashed the necks of her T-shirts, she titillated the boys with perfumed talk: here—she pointed at her pale neck—it was Loulou by Cacharel, but there, at the small of her back, she was more Dior, Poison.

While she exuded all the knowhow of a pro in femininity, Yonasz loved girls who yelped with glee if they scored at handball, the complainers, the bad losers at Risk on Wednesday afternoons, those who spoke with their mouths full and hated Phil Collins as passionately as he did.

Throughout the ninth grade, Sandra had nicknamed Yonasz "Rabbi Jacob," doing a supposedly folkloric jig whenever she came across him. He'd feigned indifference: the young girl tended to dig her teeth into those who fought back.

Delighted to be in Sandra's good books this year—she'd apparently forgotten the rabbis—Yonasz had smiled along with the others at her imitation of Cléo's haughty demeanor. As if she were gracing them with her presence . . . Her cousin had been at the same junior high as Cléo: she'd strung everyone along with some yarn about a competition, bragging about being able to introduce VIPs to anyone interested. Miss Showbiz. It was obviously bull. And her father had been unemployed forever.

The French teacher had sparked some enthusiasm by announcing that, once a month, they would do a spoken commentary on the lyrics of a song of their choice. Lots had been drawn: in October, Yonasz would team up with Cléo.

Her schedule seemed like that of an overworked adult, but they finally agreed on meeting up the following Saturday, at a café called Le Pactole.

Suggesting singers replaced any small talk. Yonasz came up with Les Rita Mitsouko, or Jacques Higelin? Or a good old Téléphone rock number? As for old stuff, his parents had everything Barbara and Brel had ever done.

Cléo didn't know Les Rita Mitsouko well, or Higelin, but they were fine by her, she listened to a bit of everything, she'd let him choose.

Everything? Impossible. No one liked everything. Liking a singer was taking a stand, it said a lot about you, preferring one style over another, it was far more than just an aesthetic choice. One COULDN'T listen to both Les Rita and Jeanne Mas! protested Yonasz. Because otherwise, what next, Neneh Cherry was Pia Zadora?

Fine, said the young girl, when pressed to give a name. There were two singers she liked better than the rest: Goldman. And Mylène Farmer. Yonasz thought Cléo was joking and burst out laughing, Cléo blushed.

He was just about to demonstrate how impossible their

collaboration would be when the young girl on the dark gray, utility-knife-scratched booth seat, had placed the palm of her hand against her chest: *here*. They gripped her heart, those songs. Jean-Jacques Goldman grabbed her right *here*, with *those things deep inside that keep us awake late*, and Mylène Farmer, too: *Dangling from the bed like a doll with dislocated limbs.*

It was clear to Cléo that Yonasz found those lines lame. But why? He'd said he liked poetry, why not this poetry?

Living in a dream from staying up so late praying to shadows and walking so much

Staggered, Yonasz decided to play along to cut things short: finding himself stuck with her really got to him, he was dying to moan to his sister about it. Just his luck. Mylène Farmer. Goldman.

When it came to Anglophone singers, Cléo mainly liked the CDs she heard at her dance classes: Janet Jackson, Madonna. They filtered right through her blood and down to her feet. Yonasz nodded, defeated. He ended with a vague joke: so they'd form a "government of cohabitation," he'd be Mitterrand and leave Chirac to her.

They came to an agreement the following Saturday, it would be Étienne Daho and his song, "Duel au Soleil."

For two weeks now, Cléo's words left hanging, her way of listening closely to him, had thrown Yonasz. Her calmness defused any debates, his need to fight and win. Cléo and her pauses broadened the horizon.

Yonasz found himself confiding his fears to her: of not being funny, being too funny, an annoying clown, having a shrill voice, anxiety about his breath, his eyebrows, his dread of brushing against a girl's thigh, or of not doing so and being called gay. He was surprised to hear himself imagining his own future in front of Cléo: he'd pass his *baccalauréat* with flying colors, become a criminal lawyer or a journalist for this great fanzine, *Les Inrockuptibles*. He'd live in a studio in the heart of Paris, go to the movies four times a week, and learn to play bass guitar on the weekends.

Yonasz tapped on his big sister Clara's bedroom door, keen to get a diagnosis: was he in love? Even if he didn't have the slightest desire to see Cléo naked? After supper he'd grab the phone from the coffee table in the sitting room, stretch the corkscrew cord to his room, close the door and dial her number, or wait for her to call.

The other pupils had, at first, been amused by their increasing closeness, commenting on the strange team they made, the nerd and the dancer; they sat side by side in class, lunched face-to-face in the cafeteria, and parted with a *Speak tonight*. Yonasz curtly rebuffed those who wanted to know: did Cléo go all the way?

They would have liked them to be lovers, or gays pretending to be a couple, but they didn't even have the grace to do that. It was so boring, their virtuous friendship, like they were in fifth grade. By the end of October, both had ceased to be of any interest to their classmates. Sandra and her gang excluded them from their parties and secrets: can't expect a thing from Yonasz, he's turned on by cheap starlets, everyone knows that Jews are attracted to all that glitters. Even when it's fake.

All the girls Yonasz knew danced. In grade school, their mothers gathered their hair into little buns. In middle school, tired of pink tulle and criticism, they were forever in purple woolly legwarmers over black footless tights and never missed an episode of *Fame* on TV.

Cléo imagining that she was already a professional dancer didn't bother Yonasz: he himself got pretty passionate about tennis every time Roland-Garros was broadcast, even briefly considering combining sports with studies.

She devoted her Monday, Wednesday, and Friday evenings, and every other Saturday afternoon, to dance. Spoke of the pro level and preparing for auditions. Corrected Yonasz: modern dance was different from contemporary. And what she did was modern jazz.

Full of contempt for the girls who "couldn't hack it," Cléo relished repeating the teacher's cutting remarks to him. Her ruthless glee made Yonasz feel uncomfortable, as did her childish obedience. Her dance teacher determined her mood: if he complimented her, she was exultant, if he ignored her, Cléo was in despair, what an idiot, she'd never achieve anything, ever.

While waiting to become a pro, and still declaring that getting her *baccalauréat* would be of no use to her, Cléo applied herself to handing in faultless work, and always on time. She summarized each lesson on sky-blue cards, read carefully what Yonasz merely skimmed over.

When classes had first begun, the young girl's seriousness

had made him fear that Cléo might rob him of the top grades. But hers was only seeming excellence.

Such application for barely O.K. results made him feel guilty about his own laid-back attitude, knuckling down to essay writing at 6 P.M. on a Sunday, only to be congratulated by most of the teachers.

He'd offered her his help in geography, in English, but Cléo had said no: it would be too easy. Far better to rely only on oneself.

Yonasz teased her: such wary words were those of an old lady.

A t the end of October, he warned her that he'd be away the day after next, a family gathering. There were two of them in the class who marked Yom Kippur.

She'd never heard of it. Sitting on the bench in Mermoz park, armed with a sandwich and a can of soda—they'd skipped out on the cafeteria after seeing the menu: salsify gratin and celery remoulade—he'd tried to explain: it was a Jewish religious holiday. But mainly, it was a chance to get together and . . . She stopped him: why had he just lowered his voice? He'd gone like this: "a Jewish holiday."

No, didn't at all. You did. Didn't. Did. Standing in front of him, like a conductor pinpointing the wrong notes of a player, she insisted: he had whispered. There were no Nazis in the park!

Cléo had admitted that she didn't know any Jews. Except Jean-Jacques Goldman. But her mother liked the Jews, she found them intelligent and resourceful. Slumped on the bench, Yonasz sighed: here we go!

Cléo's mother might just as well have said that they formed an elite and secretly ruled the world. Such compliments were no such thing. If Cléo wanted, Yonasz would introduce her to his aunt and uncle, they lived on welfare in the 19th arrondissement. Not tremendously resourceful. Or rich.

Here was why he'd lowered his voice. It was a reflex, after so many comments. Yonasz was tired of being Jewish. Tired of pretending to have a sense of humor, of laughing at those asides:

Jewish, him? You'd never know, he paid for his round without a fuss.

Jewish, him? He wasn't going to whine on about the camps, at least?

Sandra, the previous year, had regularly advised him to go back to "his country," Israel. He'd never set foot there. His country was Fontenay-sous-Bois, France. Every year since grade school, Yonasz found himself in front of a puzzled teacher: YONACH? YONAZE? Could they just call him Jonas? It'd be easier. Where was he from?

What Yonasz would have given to be like Cléo: indisputably French. Without that fear of being taken to task, singled out as Jewish.

When he went to friends' homes and saw family photos, Yonasz envied them. Just as he envied graves you could visit, could place flowers on.

A family reunion at his home could be held within ten square meters. There was no one left, or almost no one. They'd all died at Auschwitz. Or on the trains taking them there, no one knew, no one would ever know. Without graves: Ada, dead at seventeen years old, Milo, at nineteen, Eva, at twenty-one, Vanouch, at twenty-four or twenty-five.

A story interrupted for eternity, the writing-off of an entire generation.

Yonasz had no light-hearted anecdote to tell her; rather, she could consider this: his grandfather had ordered his father, then six years old, to let go of his hand in the line leading him to the gas chambers, so that he'd survive. His great-aunt had been killed by a bullet in the nape of her neck, because she'd spat in the face of an SS man in the streets of Lublin.

His maternal grandparents had miscalculated when substituting France for the daily persecutions in Russia and Poland, the ghettoes and the famines. This crazy confidence they'd had in a fiction, the land of Victor Hugo, of Jean Jaurès and the rights of man, of *liberté, égalité, fraternité*. Where wearing the yellow star had been made obligatory in 1942.

Yonasz's mother had learnt to shut up before even knowing how to speak; from the age of four, she knew how to introduce herself under an assumed name. She'd been hidden in barns, convents, and also in the bosom of those Protestant families in Vif-en-Isère and Chambon-sur-Lignon, in the Upper Loire.

In 1945, his grandmother, the sole survivor, had returned to her Paris apartment to find it stripped bare by the neighbors, apart from a few chipped cups and a small box containing letters and two photographs from before their departure.

Yonasz didn't want to be Jewish. Not one bit. He'd skipped history class the day the teacher was screening the documentary *Shoah*. He knew them only too well, those looks that were bound to be directed at him in a mixture of pity and annoyance: that Yid's going to start whining again, they go on and on about it, I'm sick of it.

He didn't want to talk about it anymore, either.

That's it.

Yonasz's voice was that of a man, the quivering of his bottom lip, that of a child: Cléo was right, he didn't have the courage to be Jewish.

Cléo went to talk to a few retired folks sitting nearby, handed the tissue thus obtained to Yonasz. The heavy sun skimmed the tops of the park's sweet chestnut trees, cutting short a hint of shade. Cléo spoke without hesitation, Cléo-who-had-to-prove-herself-at-the-oral urged him to be fearless, to hold his ghosts up high, she'd be there by his side.

The groundskeeper was pacing up and down the paths, ringing a little bell. Yonasz suggested that Cléo come and have supper with his parents, for Kippur.

Right on time, clutching a bunch of coral roses and with a silver dragonfly gripping her hair at her right temple, Cléo, in a short gray wool dress and black pumps, didn't look like herself. Even her voice seemed borrowed as, following Yonasz's mother's guided tour, Cléo marveled over the merest rug, asked for the name of that object, a container of hot water with a cylinder running through it: it was a copper samovar, and the tea brewed in it was strong, verging on bitter, the Russian way, she was told.

She knelt in front of the terracotta animals placed on a chest; country folk modeled these whistles in the north-west of Ukraine, each one made a different sound. The young girl brought the head of a stag, of a fox, to her lips, delighted at the shrill tremolo.

At the table, Cléo tasted everything with rapture, had a sip of the ice-cold, unclouded vodka aperitif, declared the marinated herring on blackish bread sprinkled with cumin seeds "very salty but very good," had seconds of broth, asked for the recipes of the chopped chicken liver garnished with fried onions and the stuffed carp in aspic.

If Clara had been there—she was in Brussels, thereby escaping this interminable meal—she certainly would have given Yonasz a kick under the table: their father was loving it, overjoyed at finding an eager, amazed listener.

The twenty-five-hour ritual fast that preceded this meal wasn't an act of contrition, Serge explained, but a personal stock-taking. Time to silence our daily cacophony. Time to face up to what our silences concealed. Cléo stammered that she was really sorry, she hadn't fasted today, she didn't know . . .

No problem! Today, at this table, Serge continued, they were equal, no one was "good" or "bad": if you thought you'd done something wrong, nothing was irreparable, and if your conscience was clear, maybe you hadn't reflected enough. No religious authority could wipe away our faults. That task was incumbent upon us.

Did Cléo know the origin of the word "pardon"? It came from the Latin *donare*, to give, and *per-*, completely. Pardoning was an act of total self-denial. Of renouncing making someone pay for what they'd done. Of course, the past was irreversible. Nothing, no pardon, could undo what had happened. But "Kippur" came from *Kappar*: to cover. And not to wipe away. Pardoning wasn't forgetting. The offence didn't disappear like a stain on fabric. Any more than it was temporarily "covered over" by the pardon. Pardoning was a decision, that of renouncing making the other pay. Or making oneself pay.

There was an extraordinary text Serge would like to get Cléo to read; this . . .

Yonasz had interrupted him: "this speeded-up and yet super boring lesson on Kippur was given to you by Serge," but Cléo had protested: for once she had the chance to learn something interesting!

As she was leaving, Serge disappeared into his study for a few moments, returning with a piece of paper that he handed to the young girl.

Yonasz had accompanied her to the bus stop. They walked along a street lined by buildings with brown Plexiglas balconies, shielded from prying eyes by clumps of conifers, copses: Cléo liked this neighborhood. And the ritual candles. And the cinnamon in the meatballs. And his father was fascinating. She must have seemed really stupid to him. Yonasz didn't realize how lucky he was . . . So many words were exchanged between them at that table. She tried to make out what was written on the paper under a streetlamp, "If we weren't pardoned . . . we would be condemned to wander without strength and without purpose, each one in the darkness of their solitary heart." He pulled at her arm, she was going to miss the last 325, she pulled away, annoyed, she couldn't care less, she'd walk.

She couldn't wait to jot down in her journal what she thought she'd understood about Kippur . . . Even their jokes were interesting, special; what was it again that his mother had said? That children were the symptoms of their parents? Yonasz rolled his eyes: that came from the popular pediatrician Françoise Dolto, not his mother. But, yes, when it came to chattering, his parents were experts. He felt like he lived in a lecture hall.

The following day, Yonasz's father had declared that Cléo intrigued him. Her daily life as a trainee dancer sounded more like that of a lion tamer to him. That time she'd explained that her exceptional flexibility was a blessing as well as a threat, and that she had to strengthen herself, keep herself "in check." Like one sends a lion back into its cage. That way she had of slapping her thigh and calling herself a great lump. She was driven by something powerful, that kid, and concerning, too.

Yonasz sometimes found that his father's work as a translator rubbed off on him: he scanned people like he did texts, preoccupied with spotting any contradictions or double meanings. Cléo had been duly scanned.

Yonasz would never have described her as "powerful." In class, she whispered in his ear the questions she didn't dare ask. She greeted classmates she knew despised her, Sandra and her gang. She seemed to be prolonging a childlike state, astounded when Yonasz teased her by mentioning that a senior boy had declared that Cléo was his type.

As for Cléo's type, it seemed to be Yonasz's parents and their story, from the epic of his Polish grandmother to the recipe for apple strudel to the books Serge recommended to her.

Serge had circled June 23 in red on the kitchen calendar: they would all go, as a family, to watch Cléo's gala. Yonasz's mother raved to Cléo about the bracing effect of the Atlantic Ocean, she'd never been to the Basque Country? She should come along with them this summer, their vacation rental was small, but she could sleep on the sofa. Cléo dined with them on Friday evenings, for the Sabbath. She held out her plate as though famished.

On Sunday, they worked on their presentation in Yonasz's bedroom—the young girl was keen to do anything that postponed her time to leave: helping his sister repair a rickety shelf, sorting out some old magazines his mother had left in a pile in the sitting room.

She told Serge (she called him by his first name, as she did Yonasz's mother, Danuta) how she was getting on with her reading; this book had touched her *here*, right in the heart: Primo Levi had met his future wife, Lucia Morpurgo, at a Jewish New Year's party in 1946, and Lucia Morpurgo had offered to teach him to dance. Dancing to bring oneself back to life.

Yonasz was surprised she'd not spoken to him about this book, Cléo apologized, she'd feared he'd think it "dumb." Like the songs she liked.

At 11 P.M., she thanked them for everything, carefully folded a new text Serge had prepared for her, she'd get the last bus, her parents weren't the sort to worry.

Fond-memory-Cléo, until that day in the cafeteria when, sitting opposite Yonasz, she'd frowned, visibly disturbed by the sight of him cutting into a pork chop. She'd waited until they'd left the cafeteria, that orchestra of forks clattering against plates, knocked-over glasses of water, and names shouted from one table to another.

It was one thing not wanting to say he was Jewish, but quite another not respecting traditions. Even if he was a nonbeliever, following the rules was a way of showing his solidarity with those who'd died for being Jewish. By eating pork, Yonasz was shirking his responsibilities. And also, as she had recently read: traditions brought the sacred into the profane.

The discussion became heated. Yonasz, taken aback, cited his family's secularity for two generations, no one went to the synagogue or ate kosher! As for solidarity, if he might just have a break from it while he had lunch . . .

In Cléo's voice, he could hear his father's, that same sententious and strict tone. No. One couldn't choose when to show solidarity. It would be too easy.

Well, he wouldn't mind a bit of easiness right now. All that for a bit of pork! He preferred her at the start of their friendship, when she was singing the praises of Mylène Farmer and Drucker's *Champs-Élysées* to him.

So that's how you see me, then, she'd muttered. An idiot. Ignorant. Perfectly nice. Who says yes to everything. Someone you can just shut up if she gives her opinion.

Not at all, he was happy that she felt good in his home, that she was interested in all that, but he'd have really liked to meet her parents, too, her little brother, see her room, the surroundings she'd grown up in. It interested him. More than recalling his great-uncle's camp number did.

Yonasz had thrown in that last bit out of bravado, to put an end to this sermon. The bell was ringing, the pupils jostling to get into the overheated classroom. Cléo, with neck and cheeks mottled crimson and chest heaving, had gone hoarse, her voice strangled, tears in her eyes: sickening, that joke. She went to sit alone, at the back of the classroom.

It was in his sister that he confided. He just didn't get it. Cléo had become more Jewish than he'd ever been, and all in the space of barely a few weeks. Cléo was accusing him of not respecting a tragedy that was unknown to her.

His sister loved nothing better than those TV movies in which a sweet young girl secretly plots the murder of her roommate: Cléo gave her the creeps a bit, the way she revered the whole family. Couldn't he see how wobbly everything about her was? And she wasn't talking about her precious ankles! The look in her eyes when their father was pontificating. That thirst, that need, without knowing exactly what they were about. Was she an orphan?

The following morning, in the mailbox, Yonasz found a bag of golden caramels, his favorite, along with half a page torn from an exercise book and signed Cléo, with no other explanation.

The milky sweetness of the candies soothed him, he'd been wrong to give so much importance to that pork business. There she was, in front of the gate, ponytail standing to attention and dance bag hanging from shoulder. He expected an apology from her, which didn't come, and a heavy silence settled between them. Yonasz felt as if her usual perfume, that mix of synthetic coconut and camphor, was overpowering him, catching in his throat, even.

Had she fallen into a vat of monoi oil this morning, or what? It gave him a migraine, that minimart smell. Cléo remained impassive, the void between them echoing with his words. At recess, she asked about Friday-night supper: 7:30, as usual? Yonasz lied, blatantly: his parents had family coming round, there wouldn't be enough space around the table, sorry.

Has your servant dumped you? asked Sandra, seeing him alone at the bus stop, Cléo having opted to walk home.

It was he who'd dumped the servant. They weren't married.

She didn't ask why they'd fallen out. But admitted being relieved: smart as Yonasz was, he had no business being with a girl like her, he'd taken his time realizing it. Yonasz knew, of course, about Cléo? No? Oh, Sandra was all for knowing what you wanted in life. But there were limits. Sandra, she had morals. At middle school, Cléo hadn't ONLY worked on her dancing. If Yonasz saw what she meant. That grant of hers, for excellence, it was mainly for the excellence of her ass, displayed to showbiz oldies, who'd "helped" her in return. At thirteen years old. YUCK. Okay, we all make mistakes. But Cléo's current disguise as little miss perfect . . . what a joke!

How had he ended up saying it? Joining in, without even being asked to, in tearing Cléo to pieces? And with such ease, he'd hardly felt a twinge in the pit of his stomach, or any hesitation when he'd gone even further: well, that explained everything. Cléo was trying to seduce his father. It was gross. That's why they'd fallen out.

Yonasz walked the dreary streets buoyed by a new exhilaration, the thrill of discovering a casual cruelty within himself, similar to Sandra's. No longer would she call him "Rabbi Jacob."

As the discomfort of his betrayal reared up, he pushed it away by quickening his step, by being his own counsel, claiming imaginary insults: Cléo had humiliated him. She'd lied to him, had never mentioned any kind of grant. She, too, spoke of her past in a hushed voice, in a voice so faint he hadn't detected a thing.

All that he'd liked about her exasperated him. She let physiotherapists twist her in two, and was delighted to be belittled by dance teachers in the name of "Art." Her over-plucked eyebrows, the way she said "dunno" for "I don't know," her indiscriminate passions, liking Kool & the Gang as much as Depeche Mode, as long as it touched her *here*. Her desire to do well at school.

It was open season, and it was he who'd sounded the horn. His childhood was behind him.

On Monday morning, these words, written in dark-blue felt-tipped pen, on the plastic of the tables and the wood of the two benches in the schoolyard: CLÉO SUCKS OFF OLD MEN.

A refrain that Sandra chanted whenever Cléo went by: CLÉO SUCKS OFF YONASZ'S FATHER.

Cléo had phoned him late that evening, *Am I disturbing you?* Yonasz did know that this was nonsense, didn't he? His father . . . The shame. When he was so . . . different. Yonasz heard Cléo blowing her nose at the other end of the line. Her gasping whispers, those of an animal being strangled until its tiny vertebrae, like jacks, could be felt. Just wait a bit, it'll blow over, Sandra will tire of it, Yonasz reassured her.

Within a few days, the machine that had so impressed his father had broken down. She'd sprained her ankle getting off the bus and would have to stop dancing for two weeks. She went to the wrong classroom, forgot to hand in an essay, asked to go to the infirmary for a stomachache, a headache. No longer lunched in the cafeteria, didn't eat lunch at all. At recess, in the afternoon, she went out to buy herself a packet of chocolate Prince cookies. Stuffed them into her mouth, one after the other: her hand automatically plunged into the packet while she was still masticating a mush of sugar and flour. To his sister, Yonasz said that Cléo wasn't "in great shape," there'd been "some issues" with Sandra, not mentioning the way he'd crumpled the taut gossamer of their friendship, a fabric that had flapped with all the flamboyance of a flag, allowing the world to be seen through it, but protecting them from the world, too.

He'd announced to his parents that they wouldn't be seeing her on Friday, or Sunday. To his father, who was anxious to know whether they'd fallen out, Yonasz replied that it was just the way things went, they weren't going to spend their lives together, and anyhow, Cléo was invasive. For a brief moment, his father looked at him, man to man: *So, you're a customs officer now, you have borders to protect?* he retorted, drily, before leaving to shut himself up in his study again.

As he'd predicted to Cléo, Sandra only taunted her for about a fortnight. Her revelations hadn't had the seismic effect she'd hoped for, leaving most pupils either indifferent, or incredulous: Cléo with the baby face and ponytail, a slut in eighth grade? Yeah, sure.

The trajectory of Yonasz's and Cléo's friendship went backwards: they said hi at the school gates, he passed on his parents' greetings, she thanked him with the courtesy of a diplomat. On the day of the presentation, they each analyzed verses of Daho's song. *Caught in a trap you'll surrender.* The French teacher congratulated them on their fine teamwork.

At the beginning of April, Yonasz invited Gaëlle, whom he'd been dating for two weeks, to a dance show at the Théâtre de la Ville. He'd kept the tickets safe in his notebook since January, a surprise he had in store for Cléo. Gaëlle was good-humored in all circumstances, as much when she'd helped him put on a condom as when he'd been unable to penetrate her: with her, nothing was a big deal. Yonasz's sister found her "bland," but still preferred her to the girl she still called Cléo-the-psycho.

In Yonasz's amorous history, Gaëlle would feature as his "first serious relationship." He would associate the discovery of sex with the steadiness of their relationship: they went to the movies on Wednesday afternoons, had a croque-monsieur for supper at the café, and then slept together, always in that order.

Some mornings, Yonasz woke up with his heart pounding, like a fugitive.

On the last day of term, their main teacher had asked them what they had each learnt of importance during this first year of high school.

Yonasz could have replied that he'd gained a new awareness of himself: he wasn't that "big galoot" with light-green eyes whose awkwardness touched his mother. He wasn't that alt-rock fan whose opinion older boys sought out: the Beastie Boys, any good?

His father had got it right: he was just a customs officer

concerned with borders, boundaries, who'd punished Cléo for having stepped beyond those of his cowardice. He'd abandoned her to those who marched, arm in arm, down the school corridors, CLÉO SUCKS OFF OLD MEN. He'd rid himself of Mylène Farmer and Jean-Jacques Goldman. Of Cléo, who made him close his eyes when crossing the road to prove his trust in her.

When he announced to his parents that Cléo was moving to the Lycée Racine, in Paris, to specialize in dance, his father asked him for her address. He'd promised her a piece on forgiveness by the philosopher Jankélévitch, and a poem by Musset, he wouldn't break his word. It was a matter of principle.

In 1989, Yonasz just missed getting the top grade for his *baccalauréat* by two-tenths of a point. In July, on the Champs-Élysées, he met an English girl, there, like him, to watch the parade designed by Jean-Paul Goude marking the bicentenary of the French Revolution. He enrolled to study law, moved into a flat-share in central Paris, as he'd predicted to Cléo. He seldom went to the movies, promised himself he'd learn to play the bass guitar soon.

Yonasz, Clara, and their mother called each other every night. None of them cried, they listed things to do: bring Serge his Discman, he missed his music at the hospital. He'd soon run out of books to read. Make another appointment with the doctor: this new chemo exhausted Serge; they could bake him a zucchini cake, it was easy to eat.

His father, on a constant morphine drip, asked for news of Gaëlle, sighed that she was really dull, what a shame Yonasz hadn't been good enough for Cléo. Actually, he had to finish writing to her: Serge propped himself up on his pillows and, with his fingertips, traced giant letters in the air.

One Thursday in May 1990, in the large Nanterre lecture hall, Yonasz's history professor announced that, in light of the news, the course would be modified. He would speak that morning of the anti-Jewish laws of 1940 and of French anti-Semitism. But first, they would observe a minute's silence.

Barely thirty seconds had passed before Yonasz felt nausea sweep over him; the girl sitting beside him was drawing little squares on her paper, and yawning.

He got up. He didn't want this silence. Or this lecture. Indeed, they were both intimately linked, history and silence. What he did want was to write a name on the board and for it to be read out loud: Monsieur Félix Germon. Having died fifteen days ago, he'd been buried in the Jewish cemetery of Carpentras. Disinterred, dragged out of his coffin, the naked corpse of an octogenarian, dislocated, lying face down on the smashed tomb, with, between his legs, a parasol stake, a simulation of impalement.

The thirty-four Jewish graves desecrated in Carpentras were headline news in the daily papers.

It was a Monday, and they were all walking slowly, having stood around for hours; the streetlamps of Paris had just come on, an orangey halo contradicting the night. His sister was holding his hand, like when they were kids. If he let go for just a moment, when a demonstrator got in the way, she immediately grabbed hold of his fingers again. It was good, their mother repeated, really good that there were no slogans at all. Her tears left colorless meandering traces on her cheeks.

Yonasz had spotted the figure of François Mitterrand among a line-up of gray suits: those of Georges Marchais, Pierre Mauroy, and Alain Juppé, and behind them, the sky-blue suit of Danielle Mitterrand.

The demonstration was drawing to a close, but no one was leaving the procession, they would keep walking, wordlessly, but they must keep walking. When the march was crossing Place de la République, a few individuals darted off to tag the brasserie Chez Jenny, which hosted meetings of the Front National. His sister encouraged them with whistles: BRAVO! Where do you think you are, at a far-left demonstration? her mother had muttered. That's right, let the Nazis gather for a drink, let's stay discreet, let's not complain, Clara had screamed: for her, the time for hiding was over.

Yonasz was trying to hold his sister back when he saw a hand waving in his direction. Then, with hair swaying and a little crimson scarf knotted at her neck, she was hurrying towards them: Cléo. She took Danuta's hand, and Clara's. And Serge? He hadn't come along? Yonasz informed her of his death, she brought her hand to her heart: not Serge, not Serge. Cléo hugged Yonasz tight, he didn't recall her being so tall. The girl who, one afternoon, in the park, had told him not to be ashamed: a strong child who was calling him to life.

When she half-opened her notebook, in class, Yonasz sometimes glimpsed pages covered in his father's handwriting. One day, the young man had offered his help: they couldn't be easy to read, these tales of forgiveness. Cléo had stretched her legs under the table, turned her ankles in, out, before replying to him: thanks, she'd manage on her own.

■ ■ ■

To the sender of the email, whose name is unknown to him, verylucie@free.fr, Yonasz writes the following: Cléo is indeed his "fond memory 1987," but he's not sure that he is hers.

3

The blue envelope, received the previous day, is attached with a paperclip to the cover of the day planner on a desk scattered with prescriptions and Post-it notes scribbled with first names to remember.

This mess is testimony to Ossip's continued presence in his clinic: first appointment 7:30 A.M., last patient 9:30 P.M., including Saturdays. He approaches time with mathematical rigor: mornings are reserved for priority cases, the sprain of one patient the day before a premiere, the pulled muscle of another in the week of a competition. Ossip keeps his afternoons and evenings for pains that still allow their sufferers to keep dancing.

■ ■ ■

It was by chance that, thirty years ago, dancers had found their way to him: a young girl lived in the building where Ossip quietly provided local physiotherapy, mainly for office workers' lumbago. She had come to find him one Saturday morning, panic-stricken: she had just injured herself during a rehearsal and was competing for the Lausanne international dance prize in a few days' time. When he had presented his diagnosis—it was impossible for her quadriceps to mend that fast—she had stopped him with three imperious words: she must dance. It was up to him to sort it out.

Since then, he had learnt to silence his anatomical objectivity in front of these creatures whom nothing could convince: they must dance.

At first, he spoke to them as if to children one keeps telling not to cross the road before the little man turns green. Don't take too many painkillers. Or anti-inflammatories.

Then, as the years went by, he had resigned himself to being a mere mechanic, just good for sticking repair patches onto worn-out mechanisms. They must: Ossip complied. The dancers were completely mad, and Ossip was madly in love.

His wife worried about him being surrounded by dragonfly-girls with concave abdomens, slender arms, and unobtrusive busts. What he mainly saw, he had reassured Lydia, was deformed feet, muscular backs, and ankles swollen with synovial fluid, dark shadows under eyes and pale lips due to dietary privations.

He forced himself to jot down, in a notebook, the vocabulary of an unknown language: a relevé was done on one leg, a développé in second position used the hamstring muscles. But the words logged revealed nothing to him, and Ossip found it infuriating not being able to visualize what his patients were describing to him, how exactly they had injured themselves.

Maybe he could go and watch a class? Lydia suggested. He asked two or three girls about this: since they enquired as to the age of the child who was to start dancing, he tried to seem as casual as possible: the child was him.

He had gone to the Repetto store the way one might half-open the door to a sex shop, embarrassed to find himself in the middle of a clientele of slight little girls and their mothers.

Gift wrap wouldn't be necessary, he told the salesgirl: the black Lycra tights, black size-ten ballet shoes, and white T-shirt would be his. He was forty-five years old.

To an astonished Lydia, he announced that he would close the clinic earlier on Wednesday to go to the dance center in the

Marais. It was time to complete his training. Watching would teach him nothing, he needed to feel it.

The men's changing rooms were almost empty, apart from two adolescents and a small boy in the same tights as Ossip.

Finding himself confronted by his own clumsiness was a kind of torture. The mirror coldly reflected back the image of his tense shoulders, up around his ears, and his knock knees. Prompted by a Chopin waltz, he launched himself forward: for a brief moment, joy coursed through him, until he caught sight of his grotesque, panting reflection, as it stumbled. The young and energetic ballet teacher, Anna, hoisted his leg up forty-five degrees while looking at her watch: the muscle fibers relaxed after ninety seconds. Ossip didn't contradict any of her dubious anatomical claims, he gave himself up to rituals that were a century-and-a-half old. Just like millions of hearts before, his had soared when Anna encouraged him with a *Not too bad, keep going, Ossip!* The young pupils congratulated him—at his age, pretty impressive. Ossip had become their mascot.

He had shooting pains in his right meniscus upon waking, the arching tortured his lower back, and he was terrified a tendon might give way, like an over-taut string.

He had lasted an entire year and then bowed out: he'd started thirty-five years too late. He carefully folded the black tights and put the ballet shoes away in a drawer, feeling a sadness that merely increased his passion for them, his dancers who battled on in a land he didn't belong in.

When he went to applaud them performing on stage, he held his breath as he watched them moving around, like a designer anxious about the seams of a splendid dress. As they took their bows, he was so overcome with emotion that he disguised his sobs as a coughing fit, so Lydia wouldn't notice.

Ossip pampered them: he covered the examination table with a warmed towel and played quiet music on FIP radio;

in the waiting room, every morning, he sprayed an orange-blossom room scent. On the coffee table, *Beaux-Arts Magazine* and *Danser* replaced celebrity magazines.

He was father to a sisterhood with long necks, big eyes, and hair that, having escaped from its elastic by late afternoon, floated like silk thread. He sometimes got them mixed up, Amandine, Alexandra, and their mothers in the waiting room, who greeted him effusively.

It was easy to imagine the setting of those particular child-hoods: Haussmann buildings with entrance halls and wide, silent stairs covered in dark-green carpets, Sunday walks in the Jardin du Luxembourg and matinées at the Théâtre des Champs-Élysées, holiday homes, and nannies who were "part of the family."

As for her, everything set her apart from the others, starting with her name, light as a pet name: Betty. She was seventeen when he treated her for the first time.

She had held out long, bony fingers with short nails to him; it was May, and she wore denim Bermuda shorts and a sky-blue short-sleeved blouse with a white collar, which brought out her bronze skin. Her slight lisp contrasting with her 1m 76cm height, Betty was polite like a kid, calling him sir when they all called him Ossip, and apologizing profusely for being just min-utes late.

Betty explained, without any vanity, that her teachers at the conservatoire, along with her fiancé, predicted that she'd be hired in the corps de ballet of a large company before the autumn. Her progress demanded respect: she may have started dancing in an ordinary, suburban youth and culture center and had very few private lessons, but she had won medals at sev-eral national and even international competitions.

After four sessions, Ossip started to dread her coming, so inept had her case made him feel. As soon as he resolved one pain, another sprang up. Of course, the connection between various ailments was well known: tendonitis of the knee might trigger lower back pain, and pulling the quadriceps might prompt pyramidal syndrome. But Betty's body had no respect for logic. And if, as Ossip put it, the body "spoke" and one just needed to listen to it, then her body's speech was incoherent.

Her shoulder had seized up. How had she injured herself? No idea. A sharp pain along the shin would strike in the middle of the night. Three days later, it had disappeared, but at the back of her neck, well . . . Ossip had returned to manuals he hadn't consulted for about ten years, and confided in the psychologist with whom he shared the clinic: he had suggested that Betty call him. Ossip hadn't dared mention it to the young girl.

They both looked for a clue in her sleep pattern, her diet; Betty stretched out her long brown legs on the table, looking skeptical: she drank a liter-and-a-half of water a day, ate lightly, and went to bed before midnight. Her fiancé couldn't understand it, either, and yet he'd known her for years and years.

One morning, Betty had given him a little package tied with ribbon: chocolates. She'd just celebrated her eighteenth birthday and had auditioned for the Opéra de Bordeaux, successfully.

Ossip didn't really take offense at not hearing from his former patients, as he repeatedly told Lydia: his titanium dragonflies were keen to forget him, both him and all his exercises.

A year and a half later, she had resurfaced on his answering machine, *hello sir it's Betty I don't know if you remember.*

Betty was the same as ever: she tilted her head to try to see the photos on the walls of his storeroom when he popped into it for a towel; bit her nails and got annoyed with herself for doing so; quoted her fiancé; turned her back to him to get dressed.

The Opéra de Bordeaux? She'd almost never performed on stage, confined to being an understudy. Despite the choreographer's compliments on her technique, her presence, her grace, she was only there to fill in when another dancer was tired, a soloist suddenly injured. A Miss "Just-in-Case." Second best.

Ossip didn't recognize this bitter tone, this weary irony in her.

The seventeen-year-old Betty dreamt of the great classical roles, of sylphides and swans. The nineteen-year-old one did the rounds of auditions for ads and fashion: one had to eat. As she lay on the treatment table, twice a week, Betty went through the brands as one does one's address book, a review of both those that were loyal and those fickle. For Nike, she'd pretend to play basketball. For Narta, the thirty-odd Nordic-looking dancers in the waiting room put her off staying at the casting. Same thing for Evian: it wasn't specified in the notice, but everyone knew it, the dancers hired would invariably be blond. Drinking water and smelling good seemed to be reserved for whites. She sighed as Ossip applied electrodes to her lower back. *Do you know what I mean, sir?*

Once she had left, he had remained for a few moments in the silence of the storeroom, where he kept admin files, clean towels, and treatment products. The walls were plastered in signed photos. *To Ossip, with all my gratitude. With all my thanks.*

Your storeroom's a cenotaph, your life a museum, his wife teased him. In the confined air of the small room there wafted a scent of violets, of old-world sweetness, a candle given by a girl's mother.

A friend who was a dresser at the Diamantelles cabaret had given him a square of opal-green velvet, against which Ossip had placed the photo of a Russian dancer from the Kirov Ballet (on tour, he'd needed urgent treatment for a painful hip). Captured a meter up from the ground, his back defied gravity in a perfect arc.

This was what Ossip expected from dance: that it compensate for the daily chaos of crime, disaster, financial scandal, opinion polls, and actors' indiscretions. The news was just dispensable squealing that distracted from what was essential. Ossip didn't give a damn about what was "going on," all of that would be forgotten. What alone would survive was the quest for beauty of these dedicated individuals, and he knew the painful price they paid for it.

Most of his patients would never dance the roles they'd trained so long for, and their humility was all the more magnificent for it. Betty was short on humility, and her bitterness didn't increase it. He would tell her that.

Betty had listened to him, then propped herself up on her elbows: Ossip went to the Opéra Garnier often, didn't he? What did he see on that stage? Blondes, brunettes, both light and dark, redheads, tall girls, short girls. All white. If there was surprise at that, the management pointed to an Arab star dancer and a soloist with Asian roots. So it was all fine.

Throughout her childhood, Betty had been ashamed of the contrast between her legs clad in the traditional "nude" tights and the brown of her bare arms, unworthy of a Princess Aurora. She covered them every day in a porcelain foundation, to blend in with the other girls. A chorographer had wrinkled his nose at the sight of her arriving at an audition for *Swan Lake*. As if she'd come to the wrong room. Despite all the medals won, the competitions, the congratulations, she still wasn't part of "the family."

It was unfortunate, but tradition . . ., Ossip had said, with a sigh.

Would Ossip also stick up for such a "tradition" in the world of advertising? Most agencies were looking for dancers between 1m 75cm and 1m 78cm tall, with solid technique and long hair. Betty had those attributes. Apparently, she didn't evoke the clarity of a mineral water, the fresh smell of a deodorant. Her agency sent her to castings for Tahiti shower gel, brands of couscous or rum. A casting director had been amazed she didn't dance hip-hop.

Betty wasn't Arab, or West Indian, or Tahitian. Her mother's roots were in Belize, but she was born in the Val-de-Marne and knew nothing about rap; her thing was more Bach's "Chaconne" or some Chopin. Betty was tired of hearing them all describing her negatively: *not* white. Never white enough.

Ossip went quiet, awkward at being put on the spot, and anxious to restore the harmony he cherished in his clinic. FIP radio was playing a piece by Georges Delerue, the music from *Le Mépris*.

Had Betty seen that movie? Indeed, Bardot had been a dancer, maybe Betty would become a movie actress one day, he said, placing a reassuring hand on her knee; and now, if she could push his hand away hard while exhaling deeply.

All weekend, Ossip had been checking in an encyclopedia of ballet. While there were plenty of white swans and princesses, one did still find, here and there, a few "exotic" roles in which Betty would be splendid. Moorish slaves, streetwalkers, Spanish gypsies, Persian courtesans . . . Lydia was outraged: all those clichés that ballet perpetuated. Maybe in a century's time, one would see, on the Garnier stage, a black sylphide or an Arab swan. But today, Betty had every reason to be furious. What an idea, anyhow, becoming infatuated with ballet, Lydia mocked; Betty just needed to retrain in oriental dancing. Don't you think, Ossip?

The following Thursday, Betty seemed light-hearted, her lower back was less painful, alternating between electrodes and laser treatment was producing good results. On FIP radio, the presenter was announcing the one o'clock news bulletin. Usually, Ossip lowered the volume until the music came back, but he remained beside Betty, firmly holding down the ankles of the young girl, who was lying on her front and had to raise her chest as high as possible, to test her arabesques. Ten times.

The voice of the Mayor of Paris, Jacques Chirac, combined with Ossip's ONE, TWOOO.

> How can you expect
> that
> the French worker
> who lives in the Goutte d'Or, where I walked with Alain Juppé
> last week, and who works, along with his wife, to earn around fifteen thousand francs, and who sees, piled up in the next-door flat in his housing project, a family with a father, three or four wives, and about twenty kids
> (approving murmurs from the crowd)
> and who get fifty thousand francs in welfare payments without, of course, working
> (applause from the crowd)

Ossip felt Betty's ankles shake between his hands,

> *if you add to that if you add to that the noise and the smell*
> (roars of laughter from the crowd)
> *well, the French worker next door, he goes crazy, he goes*
> *crazy, that's just how it is, and it must be understood: if you*
> *were there, you would have the same reaction, and it's not*
> *being racist to say that.*

The presenter's muffled voice announced the weather forecast, after "that forceful speech." Very appropriate, that "forceful," to what we're doing, remarked Ossip, smiling.

Betty had gotten dressed as she usually did, with her back to him. Most of the dancers pulled on their trousers unperturbed by his presence, and Betty's modesty had always moved him: that childlike way of protecting herself from the eyes of others, just as kids covered their eyes with one hand, imagining that, in so doing, they made themselves invisible.

A few days later, her mother had phoned: Betty wouldn't be able to come on Thursday. Just flagging a bit. But she'd soon be better. She was a tough one. Of course, Betty had a tendency to dramatize, as Ossip must have noticed. Betty had been a force of nature since the age of ten, she'd soon be back on track! Giving up dancing, her fiancé, everything *we* sacrificed ourselves for: no way. If you listened to young girls . . .

Lydia had comforted him: Chirac's nasty speech had nothing to do with it, Betty probably couldn't care less about aging politicians.

When he played his answering machine in the mornings and there was never a message from Betty, Ossip's heart slowed right down, that storeroom heart that loved nothing more than the old-fashioned scent of a world of traditions, from which Betty was excluded, *do you know what I mean, sir?*

The years had passed by, fluidly, a succession of seasons and injuries, caused by an under-heated rehearsal room in winter, dehydration in summer.

Ossip turned down offers from publishers and magazines alike: he had no "tricks" to share with whiners fretting about their "beach bodies."

Young physiotherapists recognized the precision of his diagnoses: when it came to dance injuries, there was nothing he didn't know. But old Ossip was also a skilled diplomat, meeting everyone's demands in order to stay in their favor: that of the dancers, whose overuse of painkillers he kept quiet about, and that of company directors, for whose managerial brutality he found excuses.

If he was reproached for this, he put it down to the "traditions" of a very special world.

No one could imagine him retiring, the man who refused to use a computer: if someone wanted to contact him, phone and post would suffice.

■ ■ ■

Ossip had read the letter in the blue envelope, received the previous week, once. He fixed it to his planner with a paperclip, promising himself to reply to it promptly.

This morning, he reread it.

A certain Robin, introducing himself as Betty's husband,

begins with a few flattering words: Ossip meant a great deal to Betty.

What follows is rather cryptic, referring to "a file to be put together over a matter concerning Betty." Two or three lines signed by Ossip would suffice, testifying to the "depressive, post-traumatic" state of his wife at the time. Robin was careful to include the precise dates of when Betty had consulted him, even enclosing a photo of her as an adolescent. Blouse with round, white collar, brown curls pulled back, those clear eyes, so confident, when, together, they were probing the causes of her injuries, an investigator at her own bedside.

Betty who had defeated him, whose indecipherable symptoms, disorders, Ossip dreaded. Betty who had exposed his world, his storeroom, with its walls cluttered with princesses in nude tights.

The blue envelope is strangely square, and as he slides it into the mailbox, Ossip feels as if he's just voted. He's at peace. It's the right decision.

4

T he scarlet letters of the message, an appeal for witnesses, linger on the screen; they will soon be replaced by the intro to the TV news. The two guests, wearing the same dark hooded sweatshirts and gray trousers, both frown when the journalist calls them by their first names, Enid and Elvire. He describes them as "post-MeToo dispensers of justice and multi-award-winners at prestigious festivals." The two women, in their forties, exchange a brief weary look, then remind viewers of the subject of their next documentary, and the email address women could write to them at if they were *aged around twelve between 1984 and 1994 and contacted by a certain Galatea Foundation.*

Alan switches the TV off. The bunches of yellow freesias at the florist's across the road say it's spring; Alan has never liked that shrill season, elbowing out muffled winter. He prefers it when the cold still makes the figures of passersby scurry along, when night comes early, with its considerate and consoling darkness. Being able to moan from its depths.

What's the dirty trick that makes one suddenly old? Incapable of remembering a name one never expected to forget. Was it Galatea? Or Athena? Cassiopeia?

Memory blanks are a symptom of male menopause. As is his struggle to get going every morning. Alan read somewhere that avoiding routine and retaining a readiness to marvel would slow the decline of his neurons.

■ ■ ■

For years, he was the one who enabled thousands of spectators to marvel. For years, routine, for Alan, looked like those girls, in every town, outside every concert hall. Little bag slung cross-body, hair tied back in velvet scrunchie, all glossy, shimmery, sugary.

Those who pretended to search in their bag when checked, they'd "forgotten" their invitation, those who knew a musician, those who claimed to know a musician, those who set their sights on Alan, or on a technician, those who heard messages directed only to them in the songs, those who felt unwell and had to be removed backstage.

Show producers nicknamed Alan "the Swiss army knife": the man who booked the train and plane tickets, the hotels, the taxis, filled in the travel documents, making sure to write his phone number clearly, followed, in capital letters, by: *AVAILABLE DAY AND NIGHT*.

He was the father, the friend, the psychologist of the bands he looked after. Hundreds of bands with cokehead drummers and bass guitarists resigned to being congratulated on their technique. Hundreds of concave-chested singers who worshipped Radiohead and took offense when compared to Indochine. Alan was used to their panicking: the sheepish guitarists who admitted to him, two hours before lift-off, that they'd forgotten their amp in a hotel room six hundred kilometers away; the singers who complained that the sound was terrible at the venue, no way would they perform in those conditions. They had to be coaxed, like stray dogs, these kids who'd gotten too famous thanks to three guitar chords, who would one day wind up as fifty-year-olds who were sick of the whole circus, signing photos of their adolescent selves.

Alan-the-Swiss-army-knife, versatile and discreet, who kept an up-to-date list of dealers supplying grass, amphetamines, sleeping pills, or painkillers at any time. Just like his list of girls who wouldn't mind ending the night with a musician, but without imagining that "something special" had happened between them—and not prostitutes, because certain singers would have been offended. Preferably students, or pretending to be. Alan would order them a taxi at dawn, and some, with shadows under their eyes, would say a faint "thanks."

The record labels praised Alan's speed at sorting out any mix-ups. "Natacha" had been one such, which he'd managed to sort out, one evening in February 1995.

Today, "Natacha" must be between forty-five and fifty years old. And the name he's looking for is, indeed, Galatea.

On February 11, 1995, it was 8 P.M. when Jeff Buckley took to the stage—no one could persuade the singer to wait ten more minutes. On the pavement of the Boulevard Voltaire, the security guard was struggling to control the crush of spectators, all anxiously brandishing their tickets, dismayed at hearing, from the hall, the first bars of "Last Goodbye." Alan was just settling down to enjoy the concert from the sound-control area when he'd received an urgent call from Buckley's French agent, four words crackling out of the walkie-talkie: big / problem / outside / urgent.

Gawkers were gathering around a young girl on the ground, she was rubbing her knee, someone had picked up her keys, which had fallen out of her navy-blue knapsack, was she hurt? As for the security guard, he was ranting: playing the victim when she'd given him a kick in the shin! He hadn't pushed her hard, she was play acting! And she didn't have a ticket. A young man was shaking his head, she'd told him again and again, she'd *won* her ticket, in the Oui FM competition, it was waiting for her at the ticket office! Another, motorcycle helmet in hand, pointed at the girl and sniggered: well, you're a right cranky one, darlin'!

There was a collective *OH* when the girl leapt to her feet and shoved the guy with disconcerting efficiency, causing him to stumble against the trash can behind him. Just as the biker was shouting *stupid bitch* and the security guard was grabbing the girl by the waist, Alan intervened, anxious to avoid a complaint of aggravated assault. She must come inside, he'd find her a spare ticket, if she really didn't have one.

She'd stayed beside the sound system while the hall emptied, her hair, up in a ponytail, caught in the scarf she'd kept on. "Natacha" had hesitated a few seconds before revealing her name to him, one Alan presumed was false, but he took no offence. She'd thanked him, apologizing that she couldn't talk about the concert "right now," she was still "under its effect." He couldn't have said whether she was pretty—he was so used to beauty being heavily reinforced with lipstick and eyeliner. She was pretty enough, without wanting to draw attention to it, which was refreshing. He took her at her word: if she couldn't talk about the concert right now, did that mean she'd be able to, a bit later on?

They'd ordered a hot chocolate and a beer in the brasserie next to the Bataclan. Perched on the edge of the booth, she'd untied her ponytail with a sigh of relief, as though getting ready for bed. Her hair was the brown of polished wood with a hint of shimmery softness at the temples, and her eyebrows, fine and slightly downturned, gave her a sweet puppy-dog look.

He had questioned her: most girls marveled if a man just showed interest in them.

Where in Paris did she live, was she a student? "Natacha" had frowned, what was he, a cop? Alan resorted to a game, a way for two people to get to know one another: admit to four fears each.

Convinced that girls found an ill-shaven forty-year-old admitting to a little boy's fears endearing, Alan had listed spiders, cellars, movies with the killer inside the house, and thunderstorms.

She had started with a trite "fear of everything," and then, when he protested that wasn't fair, had added the usual snakes, cockroaches, and other insects, but ended with something unusual: she feared the kindness of people she didn't know well. Kindness handed out like some flyer for a church service, you always wondered what the price would be. Alan had found this quip stimulating, her sharp wit contrasting with her scruffy appearance, the formlessness of layers of woolens, socks pulled up over black tights, bomber jacket, and gray mittens. There was a graceful instability about her, a suggestion of imbalance.

"Natacha" appeared to have the whole night ahead of her, he should have been delighted, but the following morning he was getting the train at 6:50 A.M. to Strasbourg, the morning after that to Rennes, and then straight on to Toulouse.

How about if they went outside for a walk? She agreed, leaving him to choose the area, anywhere was fine by her; Alan had suggested Montmartre, at that time they could walk free of tourists, his motorbike was parked nearby, behind the Bataclan.

They'd go up Rue Lepic as far as Rue des Saules, avoiding Place du Tertre, where touts would try to lure them into a restaurant with tables covered in cloths stiff with spilt beer, Alan had lived in the area for about ten years. Just nearby.

As soon as he'd said them, the words struck him at their crudest: an invitation, as if she owed him something. Mumbling, garbled explanations, the more Alan spoke, the more any sexual potential lost its appeal, but "Natacha" didn't seem offended and stopped in front of the high railings of Square Louise-Michel, from which the wan floodlights surrounded the Sacré-Coeur: wouldn't it be great to be alone inside there?

At first, like a coward, he'd spoken of the groundskeepers and his weak ankles, the railing was high, after all.

Not a groundskeeper on the horizon, it was nearly 1 A.M.,

and this kind of railing wasn't hard to climb, she objected to him. She held out her hand without mocking his cowardice as he crouched on the stretch of low wall, gripping a wrought-iron ring.

She had jumped from a height of more than a meter.

She was nosing around like a kid, studying the tags, the words scrawled on the stone in marker, wrinkling her nose when she came across a syringe, an empty bottle of codeine, pointing out to him a used condom—gross. With her nose buried in her red scarf, standing on a bench, she pretended to walk along a beam, toes pointed, arms outstretched.

She was twenty-three. Alan had been amazed, he'd have said she was seventeen, eighteen. Instantly, she'd rooted around in her bag and pulled out a battered identity card, she had her driving license, too, if that wasn't enough for him.

She was quickening her step towards the exit, kicking at a cola can, with brambles caught on her trousers, soil on the elbows of her coat; he'd called out to her, hey, no way, don't you dare abandon me alone in the dark!

He'd managed to get them to sit down for a moment; having to scale the railings once again worried him, he was starting to feel cold, but "Natacha," seemingly impervious to the wintry night, was asking him questions: was Buckley anything like his music? In real life? Jeff had kept his eyes closed throughout the song "Hallelujah," was that something he did at every concert, or was it down to a particular feeling that evening?

Alan had to admit to her that, when the singer had been introduced to him, all he'd seen was a cute American and a young-girls magnet, who'd mastered the moody look to perfection in his promo photos. Then he'd heard it, that voice that critics described as "angelic," when Jeff Buckley's five octaves spanned the plains of angst.

The guy had a perfect and formidable ear. He closed his

eyes during the sound check, demanding quiet, *shut up every-body*. Went up to the mike, *mmm*, a barely sonorous murmur, and then, gradually, he opened his mouth wide, *mmmeeeeaa*, it swelled, his breath rose from diaphragm to lungs, the sound engineer hunched over the desk tried to deal with the sudden changes in volume. The empty hall resounded with his hesitations, he relentlessly repeated a line from "Hallelujah": *and love is not a victory march and love is not a*, retuning his guitar, frowning, he undressed the song, removing the vowels to pronounce only the L-N-V-M-L-N. Until the diagnosis: Jeff had just detected a high middle-register frequency that was "intolerable" at around two kilohertz, it must be sorted out immediately. That guy had swallowed one hell of a hi-fi system!

Alan realized that he was talking too much, laughing too much at his own anecdotes: at Buckley's slightest sneeze, his manager would rush to the air conditioner and cover it with a coat!

He could hear himself pontificating on singers: when they got intimations of decline, the fall to come, they clung wildly to success, endlessly calling the artistic director who was writing them off, it was so sad. Most musicians needed to be reassured about their status: that's why they asked to stay in luxury hotels and dine in Michelin-starred restaurants. Costing the labels a fortune was how they reassured themselves that they were still wanted. It was touching. Even if Alan really wanted to spank them when they complained about the "musty" smell of a five-star hotel room, threatening not to perform if somewhere better wasn't found. Annoying brats. Hookers, more like, she corrected, finally interrupting him. Yes. When one exchanged something with material value against a performance, whether sentimental or artistic, one was a hooker. It wasn't pejorative, merely objective.

He hadn't seen it coming, that sudden vehemence; she'd mocked his wide-eyed stare, what surprised him? That she'd used the word "hooker?" She was twiddling a strand of hair between finger and thumb, the way one rolls a cigarette. He couldn't imagine that this girl might have attacked the security guard.

It was past 2 A.M. when they left the park, with Alan thinking of his alarm clock that would ring at 5:30 A.M., of the travel documents to be filled in, of the taxis to be booked, of the guitars to be protected, of the following day's venue—would the acoustics be right?—of the new problems that would inevitably arise, of Buckley's tiredness, when he still had five concerts to go in France, with Alan thinking of that "somewhere else" that "Natacha" had just suggested: we could go "somewhere else"?

The young girl's springy step made him painfully conscious of his stooped back, he was just a strained stomach, bloated with too many sandwiches and pastries hastily stuffed, and the time he'd have to spend caressing her in the right place in the right way before finally getting her underwear off exhausted him in advance, his ankle hurt, he shouldn't have jumped off that wall.

When he'd opened the door to his two-room apartment, she'd admired how tidy it all was; "his" Iulia deserved all the credit for that, he said. Alan would never have thought he'd need a cleaning lady one day, but it had to be recognized that women were more meticulous than men. "Natacha" had mockingly agreed: yes, when we're paid properly, we do things well.

Would she insist on payment? Did he have any cash on him? Would a check do? The possibility that what would follow might be organized like the cleaning of his apartment made him feel better.

She'd undressed like a sportswoman before a match, quickly and without a fuss. It was sexy. That and her disguise as "Natacha." She was wearing navy-blue cotton panties and a gray bra, the mismatch was hardly appealing, maybe he was dealing with a beginner improvising for her first client? He had attempted a joke, was she a cyclist, her leg muscles were seriously defined. Alan had rushed to switch the ceiling light off and the bedside lamp on. If that was for her, he needn't bother: she was pretty keen on light.

Whispers, caresses, how beautiful she was, her collarbones, the slenderness of her neck, the softness of her thighs: "Natacha's" smile as she lay on the mustard-yellow bedspread, one leg slightly bent, seemed tinged with a polite lassitude, as if faced with an elderly gentleman going into too much detail about his day.

He'd penetrated her. Had stopped to ask if everything was O.K. She'd calmly replied: sure. "Natacha" seemed determined to give a disembodied performance, a succession of poses. Her detachment made him more conscious of his own disheveled, sweaty, groping image. His climax seemed pitiful. In the half-light, in profile, unmoved, her cheeks barely flushed, she tied up her hair again and asked for a glass of water.

And then she returned to Buckley: she'd discovered the singer when he'd appeared on the TV show, *Nulle Part Ailleurs*. Smitten as never before, here, she'd pointed her index finger at her heart, a naïve gesture, clichéd.

This emotion, granted to Jeff Buckley and totally absent from their coupling, hurt Alan, and he felt ridiculous: being jealous of a singer.

Then she said this to him, the way one announces an incurable illness: he's going to die soon, Jeff Buckley. Undaunted by his teasing—so, she was a prophet, was she?—she insisted, quoting, as proof, the lyrics of "Grace." For anyone able to listen, Buckley was announcing his death in the song: *and I feel them drown my name*. And that way of opening the concert with "Last Goodbye"?

Alan fell silent: fans just loved giving themselves the jitters by envisaging a tragic destiny for their idol. "Natacha" being a touch trite was reassuring. It was still dark when they left the apartment.

He accompanied her to the taxi stand, near the Pigalle metro station. Free of the whole sex thing, Alan had regained an energy he no longer knew he had, barely out of breath from scaling the steps of Rue Foyatier, pleased at "Natacha's" amazement in front of the Moulin de la Galette. He put on a nasal voice to indicate, like a guide, *to your left, the Moulin Rouge* and its cancan dancers, and in the Rue de Douai, further down, those tourist-swindling hostess bars, or rather, hooker bars. You're one too, you know, she retorted, without aggression. Yes, at the brasserie, Alan had explained to her that he loathed the world of fashion, but organizing a fashion show made him as much money as three or four concerts. We're all hookers, she concluded, pensively.

Maybe he'd been tactless in not paying her.

Revelers high on ecstasy were leaving the Folies Pigalle, their chemical exuberance at odds with their wan complexions. A few plainclothes policemen surrounded the entrance to the closed metro, bulky figures openly talking into the transmitters concealed in the upturned collars of their parkas.

It seemed to him like a fitting, protective gesture: Alan put one arm around her shoulders and pulled her towards him, her shoulder blades jutted out under her coat, the back of a bird. Her hair gave off a warm scent of sweets, something edible. He spotted the Place Pigalle photographer on the lookout for tourists, his Polaroid camera banging against his belly. He took the young girl's hand to pull her over to the guy: we'll have a keepsake.

No! No photo. The photographer had already turned his back on them, attracted by an approaching group of tipsy retirees from England.

Alan had joked: finally a sign, "Natacha" was married . . . Lack of sleep and the cold made him giddy, his beard was as itchy as in spring, when pollen wafted around, he felt strangely happy about nothing and everything: Buckley's incredible concert, the rave reviews that were bound to appear, the comfort of the train to come, that adolescent sleepless night, free access to "Natacha," the Sacré-Coeur and the railings scaled.

On the Boulevard de Clichy, girls with ponytails and sports bags slung on shoulders were coming out of a peep show at a brisk pace, only to push open the door of the one next door. "Natacha" indicated them with her chin: their job was to dance for exactly ten minutes facing a window. The client bought their nudity, nothing more. The deal was clear-cut on both sides. It was perfectly honest. Her fizzy laughter, by way of conclusion, was light-hearted, in total contrast with what was to follow.

She went quiet, and Alan realized that she was leaving an opening for him: "How do you know all that?" was the question he should have asked but didn't, because Alan didn't want to know: he wanted to stick with the girl who jumped over railings and brawled with the security guard.

She sat down on the cold cobblestones, under an indistinct end-of-night sky: I don't know why, but I'd like to tell you something, she said.

In any case, we'll never see each other again.

I don't know where to begin.

You don't have to, he told her, like a coward.

To begin with, she used words that Alan found touching in their vehemence, putting it down to her youth: *irreversible past, always, never, unforgiveable.*

She asked nothing of him, neither that he judge her, nor console her.

The roar of cars, the smell of sooty exhaust fumes from a tourist bus parking nearby. The shaking of "Natacha's" fingers. Her voice going hoarse. What was left unsaid. He didn't dare look at her. Not for one moment did he doubt the truth of her story. The shaking of the fingers. The voice going hoarse. What was left unsaid.

H is managerial efficiency perhaps explained his not losing the book of matches she'd agreed to write her phone number on when they'd parted at the Pigalle station.

She'd been right: Jeff Buckley had died by drowning on May 29, 1997. His body had been found on the banks of Wolf River Harbor. A walker had seen him swimming on his back, fully clothed, Jeff Buckley was humming "Whole Lotta Love." The walker hadn't been concerned, the young man seemed so calm, his voice a crystal-clear trail above the water.

Alan hadn't been invited to attend the funeral in the States.

On May 30, he had, for the first time, rung "Natacha's" number: Hi, we met at the Bataclan concert in 1995 . . .

She'd been delighted to hear "So Real" on France Inter radio that night, without realizing that . . . Really, she'd said that to him after the concert, that he'd die soon?

Maybe she didn't remember, either, what she'd confided in him, sitting right on the pavement of a Montmartre lane with uneven cobbles. When, at dawn, she'd revealed the full extent of her personal disaster to him.

They'd stayed in touch, every now and then, until 2002. The roles never changed. Alan grumbled, "Natacha" listened to him: no, live music wasn't threatened by web pirates, all due respect to show producers, who took an antispasmodic at any mention of an MP3; it was merely about to succumb to an epidemic of nesting. Insidiously, it had gone from: "Stay at home, we'll deliver pizzas, shoes, and novels to you," to: "Go home, only there will you be safe," a curfew order.

Alan might have celebrated his fifty-sixth birthday, but sharing a table with thirty-year-olds made him feel like he was dining at his grandparents': these young people got excited about those *really authentic* cement tiles they'd decorate their bathroom with, they exchanged the best "tricks" to return the shine to a coffee table. This passion they showed for "home sweet home" depressed him.

A new century was dawning in which he'd be the last not using the jargon of chefs, all those "émincés" and "duxelles," etc. The ham sandwiches at concert halls would soon be as exotic as the smell of cigarettes.

This nest obsession also contaminated love affairs. If, in the past, Alan might have feared not living up to his partners' fantasies, today he dreaded their decorator's eye. A thirtysomething woman he was lusting after had, at his place, stopped for a long time in front of a small poster for a Nirvana concert pinned to the wall. Had she talked music to him? Oh, no: she'd recommended a vintage frame store. Alan had thanked her, but never would he frame Kurt Cobain. A few days later, by text message, she'd ended their fledgling relationship: Alan suspected the thumbtacks of having let him down.

Just like when they'd met, Alan ranted on endlessly: he was working less and less, now pop stars turned up with their complete team, management included; as for more modest bands, they didn't have the means to pay for a stage manager, the sound engineer took charge of everything. And on stage, same thing: tour organizers *a-dored* duos. So cool. Not expensive. And singers just swore by multi-instrumentalists, so cool, not expensive.

Luckily, L'Oréal called on him for "events" and other conferences; marketing folk were far more docile than singers. It was utterly tedious. But . . .

You've well and truly become a hooker. There, too, I was a prophet.

Before hanging up, "Natacha" announced to him that she was "with someone," and Alan heard, maybe wrongly, that she was saying goodbye to him.

■ ■ ■

Alan half-opens the window. The rain has stopped. A message appears on his phone screen: his niece. Who'll soon be giving birth to a daughter and can't think of a name. She suspects he'll suggest something corny, but . . .

The letters jostle under his fingers, spelling out, as though obvious: Natacha. Why not Natacha?

The almost instant response of his niece—*LOL*—framed by three little faces; the first emoji crying turquoise tears of laughter, the second staring wide-eyed in astonishment, the third, its face green, vomiting a rainbow.

Seriously? That's all Alan can suggest to her? A name out of some bad TV movie? A hooker's name?

In the bathroom mirror, an old adolescent looks back at him, orphaned of a past that smelt of cold ash, like brasseries when people still smoked in them. When you scribbled a girl's phone number on a scrap of paper. When you didn't search the web for proof of the true identity of the girl you'd just met.

Today, she must be forty-eight, "Natacha," who, in February 1995, went to the Bataclan all on her own, who'd landed a kick on the security guard's shin, and who softened in full light, a stranger perfectly preserving her anonymity as a naked girl.

"Natacha," about twelve in 1985, a candidate for the Galatea grant.

5

I t's a curious thing, reopening a box of memories; you do it with confidence, certain that the past will have the touching look of a dated, quaint old thing. But the regrets prove to be intact, acute.

Even now, Lara rarely mentions Cléo. Because she can't rid that memory of its rough edges and turn it into a melancholy sweetness. Cléo remains stuck in time, a mirror held up to her faults. But hey, Lara was barely twenty at the time.

■ ■ ■

Twenty in the autumn of 1998, a student in her second year of sociology who called herself "shockingly uneducated" with the carefree frivolity of a girl returning from holiday and boasting of never wearing makeup. Lara's father said that at school, just like at uni, she got by because she lived off her cultural reserves: her parents had dragged her from galleries to shows throughout her childhood—at five she was playing hide-and-seek in the garden of the Musée Rodin and, at eight, falling asleep curled up on the gray seats of the Théâtre de la Ville.

Her mother wrote theater reviews for a glossy magazine so thick you could place a scalding-hot teapot on it without any damage.

Her reserves were not only artistic, but also political: on her father's desk, a photo of her up on his shoulders testified to her presence at the Bastille on May 10, 1981, at barely three years old.

Her parents paid her rent for the apartment she'd shared for a year. A part-time waitress in a tearoom, Lara covered the rest, which she reduced to a strict minimum: an Action-Christine loyalty card for classic movie screenings, books borrowed from the library, and, for clothes, Guerrisol, the second-hand store in Barbès.

On arrival at uni, Lara had been delighted to see so many posters for rallies; she'd attended a students' union meeting, found it terribly boring, all just infighting and politicking.

But the people she met in December, who were setting up an informal collective, as yet nameless, appealed to her precisely because they didn't "do politics": they loathed that expression. Their tracts, which they plastered all over Paris, whether on trees and buildings, got rid of the parties' deadly dull language, denounced the excessive caution of the unions, which merely "negotiated the length of the leash" on workers. They were determined to get off the established Nation–Bastille demonstration route, to have spontaneous unofficial gatherings. The previous Tuesday, fifty of them had occupied the Belleville employment office to demand benefit payment for a fifty-year-old struck off the list for not having shown enough "determination in job-seeking"; they hadn't left the place until the file was reopened, the unemployment benefit granted. That Friday, Lara had joined them at the Bon Marché store without knowing what was planned; inside, they'd picked the best Scottish salmon, the finest caviar, and several bottles of a vintage champagne. Then they'd pulled a tablecloth out of a knapsack and spread it on the ground, inviting shoppers and security guards to join them for the meal. To the flabbergasted manager, they'd handed a flyer: "You've got the dough, we've got the time." Others had filled a trolley to the brim with food and left it in front of the store's entrance: let everyone help themselves, it would soon be Christmas.

The social movement the collective was associated with was gaining momentum, a poll had revealed that sixty-three percent of French people supported what the newspapers called the "rumbling discontent" of the unemployed: the salaried were all potentially the unemployed.

To those calling for a rise in the Christmas bonus, the Minister of Labor, Martine Aubry, had just responded by awarding one franc and forty-eight centimes to those eligible.

From Nancy, Caen, and Marseilles, to Rouen, Bordeaux, and Brest, employment offices remained occupied as Christmas approached. The students gathered there found themselves joined by office workers, railroad men, nurses, teachers and "let go" executives; farm workers had come in a small delegation to show their support for the blockades dotted around France. If, at the start, the debate was only about access to benefits, now something else was the focus: people were admitting their shame at being considered "inactive," their humiliation at not having a reply to the question: "And you, what do you do?"

Lara would wake up exhausted: the demonstrations often ended after midnight, instructions were given to meet for protests from 6 A.M. onwards, and she started her shift at the tearoom at 10 A.M.

The staff at Kanel followed her activities from a distance, saved articles from *Le Parisien* for her—the collective had even made the front page with its banner, described as "anarchistic": *We want a shit job, paid peanuts.*

T he avenue on which Kanel was located, near the Pont de Neuilly metro station, was a realm of blondness, from the ladies passing by with their highlighted hair, to their mini-dogs with white and beige coats, to the lofty ochre facades of the head offices and banks.

Delphine, the manager, stressed that the tearoom's regular customers weren't just anybody: they were performers coming from the TV studios nearby. Delphine was on first-name terms with them: Mallaury and Astrid swore only by the Provençal tart, they were in the cast of *Sous le Soleil*. Janice, the backing singer of François Feldman, liked to sip a caramel tea with her chocolate tart.

Delphine's groupie ways and anxious checking of her fingertips, as if to reassure herself that her long, glossy beige nails hadn't upped and left, made her seem, touchingly, still adolescent. Her mission was to "give more style" to Kanel: art deco wallpaper adorned the walls of the restroom, and she intended to invest in a new outfit for the waitresses, a short burgundy skirt with a black taffeta bow on the hip, and a black bowling-style blouse.

Lara blew a fuse: no way was she wearing a uniform out of an American TV movie to pander to the boss's grandiose dreams. The three other waitresses, two students of her age and Christelle, who'd just celebrated her fortieth, argued that at least they wouldn't get their own clothes dirty. It was a matter of principle, Lara insisted: they weren't going to give their bodies as well as their time. Christelle had thrown her when she'd asked how a bit of fabric would make things *worse*. Lara would be fired if she didn't give in, that's what Delphine would do with her principles.

The unsold tarts she took home, the friends delighted to lunch for free on the days she did the cash register: it was the most bearable job Lara had done, compared with being a sales-girl at Agnès B. or a life-drawing model at the Beaux-Arts. If that business of the uniform would just go away.

She didn't dare admit it, but saying these words gave Lara a childish thrill: *And for you, that will be ten francs fifty, please, and twenty, which makes—anything else for you?* Here she was, being an adult, and with others believing it, believing in Lara the waitress.

Lara liked setting the cups and saucers out on the place mats, she liked the empty tearoom with chairs upended, the aroma of cinnamon and cardamom, she liked lunching at 11:15 on the previous day's leftovers, sitting at the table beside the Tamil dishwasher and the Pakistani cook.

After about ten days, Lara could tell the actors from the musicians. The former talked loudly, high on the energy they suppressed during drawn-out days of waiting around on movie sets. As for the musicians, they didn't expect anyone to recognize them.

On Fridays, a large table had to be reserved for the dancers of the Malko company, who performed in various variety TV programs. Lara thought they looked like anemic tramps, their pallid faces, those shadows under their eyes, their layers of woolens of dubious cleanliness, leg-warmers slumped around ankles, sweatpants with a baggy sweater sagging over them, necks protected with a scarf, they dragged their feet when walking, only the way they held their heads—that extended neck—was at odds with this seeming exhaustion.

One of them had left Lara his phone number; Éric hadn't seemed that bothered about the outcome, it was left up to her: if she wanted to, they'd see each other again and sleep together.

It was an agreeably odorless and smooth encounter, just like the young man's body, that toned expanse showered three times a day after rehearsals. They didn't say much to each other once clothed again, sharing a tea, a slice of cake, and a few concerns: he was looking for a veterinarian for his cat, and Lara for a roommate. The previous one, Lise, had just gone home to the States. Éric just happened to know a dancer who was looking for a room.

Everything went very smoothly. Lara called the girl, she came round the next day, armed with a folder containing her pay slips. Lara refused to look at them, awkward at being put in the position of a Delphine, of sizing up the financial reliability of a girl her own age. As proof of being serious, the young dancer listed the TV programs she appeared in, her CV: Drucker, Sabatier . . . Lara interrupted her, grinning, "razzle-dazzle variety shows" weren't really her thing, but of course, you couldn't always choose your job.

Cléo? Was it short for Cléopatre, or a tribute to Varda's film, *Cléo de 5 à 7*? Her new roommate mumbled that she didn't know the movie.

In the corridor, Cléo stopped in front of the posters pinned to the wall.

UNEMPLOYMENT IS MISERY WORK IS EXPLOITATION
WE DON'T WANT CRUMBS WE WANT THE WHOLE BAKERY
WORK IS TO LIFE WHAT PETROLEUM IS TO THE SEA

She was studying them with the attention one gives the metro map of an unknown town, and Lara found it embarrassing: this puzzled scrutiny turned her favorite slogans into a language for the initiated. Cléo apologized: she knew nothing about politics.

But had Cléo heard about the recent occupations of the employment offices? About the takeover protest at the Bon Marché? This evening, there was a gathering of the "happy unemployed" at the Jussieu campus, if she was interested. And there, they didn't speak the language of the losers we're urged to vote for, in fact, if the vote *did* change something, it would be outlawed. Cléo politely agreed and took her copy of the keys, she'd be back the day after tomorrow with her stuff.

In the morning, before her dance class, Cléo would wash her cup in a trickle of water, dry it, and return it to the shelf, she'd close the bathroom door quietly when she took her shower, wouldn't slam the door as she left the apartment. She didn't receive any calls on the landline and left no messages on the answering machine. Only her leotards and tights hanging on the line attested to her presence, along with a whiff of camphor in the bathroom. Did she eat? Probably not: inside the fridge, the same food remained in exactly the same place, no knife in the sink indicated a hastily cut bit of cheese. On Fridays and Saturdays, Lara heard the key in the lock late in the night, the other evenings, Cléo stayed in her room. Lara tapped at the door: a few friends had come round, would she join them for a drink? Cléo, sitting cross-legged on the bed, holding lined school paper, politely declined, thanks. She preferred to carry on reading.

Lara left a Post-it note on the kitchen table—*If you like, we can have supper together this evening*—which she later found with four words and three dots added: sorry am rehearsing late . . .

To those—her friends from the collective, her parents—who were surprised not to come across her, Lara responded with a sigh: NEVER share an apartment with a dancer, that girl was totally boring, nothing interested her apart from her sore feet and wiggling to Whitney Houston.

After two weeks of such a creeping presence, Lara had but one desire: to burst into Cléo's room in the middle of the night and disrupt this trail of absence, to say that this wasn't a hotel, it wasn't going to work, ciao.

She continued to serve Cléo at Kanel on Fridays and Saturday lunchtimes, but even there, they struggled to understand each other: surprised not to see her slice of tart on the check, Cléo had pointed out Lara's oversight to her. Lara had tried discreetly to make her understand—Delphine wasn't far off—that it wasn't an oversight. That evening, Cléo knocked on the door of her room: she didn't like to owe anything to anyone. She'd pay what she owed, like everyone else.

All that for a slice of zucchini tart and a cola? Such vehemence was a bit over the top, wasn't it? With what went into the cash register every day, Cléo needn't worry for Kanel. Delphine proclaimed her love of art: let her prove it by supporting dancers! Cléo shook her head, no, she didn't want any favors. None.

The following week, Lara brought the check over to Cléo, accompanied by a salted caramel: she wasn't going to turn that down, surely? Cléo blushed, a sunrise from throat to eyes.

They were starting to get used to sharing the apartment, Cléo wrote down the names of those trying to contact Lara, Lara didn't touch the packet of Tuc crackers in the cupboard: Cléo's late suppers were invariably salty and processed.

Some days seemed to be too much for Cléo. She stayed in her room, ate nothing, didn't go to classes, she was under the weather. Lara quizzed her, did she have her period? The blues? Was it something Lara had said? Cléo shook her head. She'd feel better tomorrow.

Lara's mother had seemed taken aback that she didn't know what kind of dancing Cléo did: classical ballet, modern, contemporary? She hadn't asked her? And yet, sharing day-to-day life with an artist must be interesting. Lara had then mentioned the variety TV programs, and, faced with her mother's disappointment—so Cléo wasn't a *real* dancer—Lara had added that it was bound to be temporary, just a job. She lied the way one makes up having a philosophy degree, or makes oneself younger on a CV: for her own sake.

One Saturday evening in December, at 8:30, Lara, alone in the apartment, seized the remote control, that childhood impulse: on Wednesdays, the anime series *Albator*, on Saturday evenings, *Champs-Élysées*.

The program's opening credits came with a drum roll, and, one by one, the faces of the guests were revealed on a pillar billboard, while, on the Trocadéro esplanade, the twirling dancers, whom Lara served every Friday, suddenly appeared. Michel Drucker, black bowtie and red pocket square, announced the marvels to come in a gentle, cracked voice—he seemed barely briefed, flabbergasted at the line-up: *An exceptional evening and, right away, the Ballets de Malko, amazing.*

At the back of the set, to the left of the screen, Lara didn't immediately recognize her: Cléo, expression frozen in a fixed smile that her heaving chest belied. Her tilted oval face was that of a child in an eighteenth-century painting, the refined, sweet face of a girl disguised as an adult, scantily clad in a black sequined bra and leatherette micro-shorts.

Lara had once asked Cléo how to judge the level of a dancer. On the swiftness of her movements, her suppleness, her grace? In front of the TV screen, she understood that it was something else: that ability to capture the attention, all those millions of people's attention, including Lara's. That ability to make one long to be Cléo, agile, athletic, precise, and arousing.

The closing credits scrolled across Cléo's black Lycra-clad thighs, as she clasped a platinum-blond dancer, both wearing the same glossy scarlet smile, the same fringe of false eyelashes. The camera hesitated a moment between the two of them, and then chose Cléo, zooming in on her glistening skin, cutting the dancer up into golden vignettes: breasts, thighs, fuselage of a waist in close-up, Cléo in bits and pieces, offered up to France's Saturday-night viewers.

One Monday in January, Lara got home late from a demonstration to find Cléo in the kitchen in front of a cup of tea: on the news, they had reported clashes with the police at the end of the march, were her friends O.K.? And was she?

Lara, her ankle sore from lots of running, eyes irritated by teargas, really wasn't up to choosing the words least likely to shock her far from politically savvy roommate. But the dancer asked nothing more, made her a tea, comically banging her hip on the wooden chair as she rushed to the kettle. Cléo filled a plastic bag with ice cubes, wrapped it in a tea towel, tied it around Lara's swollen ankle. Wearing childish sky-blue pajamas, she showed her bony foot to Lara, the toes like a bird's talon, demonstrating some exercises, one hundred and seven ligaments, a lot to keep in shape. She pressed her thumb into the arch of Lara's good foot; you had to press hard to release the tension; if it didn't hurt, you just hadn't rooted out the real problem. Lara smiled at her: was this maxim applicable to other aspects of her life?

As she was off to bed, Cléo popped her head round the half-opened door of Lara's room: yes, if it didn't hurt, you just hadn't dared to disturb anything.

The creature Lara watched dancing on the TV every Saturday evening, without telling her so, seemed totally divorced from her roommate. And Cléo's reserve stung her like a lie: the dancer threw lascivious glances at the singers she swirled around, and then metamorphosed into some placid girl the moment she walked through the door of the apartment.

Cléo reawakened adolescent contradictions in Lara: the yearning to be favored by the girl all the boys were after, coupled with a mistrust of the girl all the boys were after.

At fourteen, Lara had gleefully accepted a free makeover offered by a makeup expert at the Galeries Lafayette store. She could still remember the pleasure of their serious and lengthy deliberations between several shades of lipstick—scarlet, coral, wine.

When he'd opened the door to her, her father had burst out laughing: what on earth was this *tarty* look about?

Lara collected photos of the singer Vanessa Paradis, much to her parents' despair, dismayed at their daughter's *bad taste*.

At uni, it was the done thing to mock the tottering gait of students in high heels; Lara invariably stuck to black trousers, dark, baggy sweatshirt, and sneakers. The collective had drawn up a manifesto glorifying androgyny and denouncing the control imposed by diktats about femininity. Androgyny? Cléo had queried, with surprise, when she'd read it, but Lara and her friends were all dressed like the men in the collective, not the other way round: it wasn't the androgynous that prevailed, but the masculine. Were Lara's breasts a sign of inferiority?

As for Cléo, she floated from one face to another, one gender to another; on Saturday evenings, she'd remove her makeup in front of the bathroom mirror, in panties and a tank top, her triceps bulging and wrist veins prominent. The greasiness of the cream wiped away the painted smile and seductive eyes. Upon waking, Cléo still had specks of azure pigment at the corner of her eyelids.

One Sunday, Cléo had asked Lara to help her, she wanted to go redhead; wearing latex gloves, Lara had painted the dye, which stank of ammonia, onto her roommate's tilted-back head. Upside down, with hair plastered to scalp and eyes closed, Cléo looked like a cat, like a little boy.

L ara prided herself on her gift for anticipating the future, which, most often, just led to oppressive anxiety: when having supper at her parents', she announced her arrival on the intercom with a cheery "It's me, Mom," and the future death of her mother stabbed at her heart.

At a boy's first kiss, Lara visualized the break-up. When her cousin's dog nuzzled up to her, Lara shuddered: the creature's trusting look would soon be directed at the veterinarian putting it to sleep.

But when she met Cléo, Lara had no premonition, sensed nothing of what, three months later, would seem so obvious. For weeks, Lara was irritated by a roommate who was hard to figure out. Then, without stages, or progression, suddenly nothing was the same.

Lara wanted to talk about Cléo to everyone. But not by moaning about her, as she usually did. She wanted to tell Cléo's story, fly her flag.

Those dancers who performed on variety TV shows, they were working artists, without glory, she explained to her circle. The audience didn't linger on them. No one would write rave reviews on Cléo. And the best part of it, Lara enthused to her nonplussed friends, was that Cléo couldn't care less. When, in fact, all of them, in the Malko company, were incredible. So, after all, a friend pointed out to her, "spangly variety shows" *were* Lara's thing.

At what moment had the letters of Cléo's name started insinuating themselves into everything, like some joyous Scrabble game?

Someone said foot, Lara heard leg, black tights, CLÉO. Someone said pain, she thought camphor, ointment, bathroom, CLÉO CLÉO. Someone served Lara an over-steeped tea: CLÉO, in the morning, forgetting the strainer in the teapot. Some feminist friends led a march, their banner quoted the anarchist Emma Goldman, "*If I can't dance, this is not my revolution*": CLÉO CLÉO CLÉO.

It was March, and the apartment had become a theater for banal little scenarios: on Saturday, close to midnight, Lara, with all the attentiveness of a TV-movie wife, would wait up for her, welcome her, ask how Cléo's evening had gone. The choreography? Tricky? The singer? Friendly? And Drucker? In a good mood?

Sitting on the lid of the toilet in her panties, frowning, legs slightly apart, Cléo was applying balm to the bruises left by her dance partner's fingers. Lara had noticed it! That dancer with the shaved head had lifted her so aggressively!

Knowing what went on behind the scenes secured her a special place, she wasn't taken in by the Cléo with false eyelashes who flirted with the whole world.

As they both sat cross-legged on the bed, Lara carefully brushed out, one by one, the strands clogged with glittery gel. Cléo was losing patience: Lara should give a big, hard tug, they weren't going to spend all night on it. On Monday evening, after a Sunday off, Cléo stretched her leg out towards her, *Pull on my legs*, she ordered. Lara grabbed hold of her ankle and slowly moved up the dancer's leg. Cléo leaned on Lara's shoulder with one hand, Cléo, close up, had the fine, straight eyelashes of a little girl.

And finally, it had happened. Cold air was coming in

through the room's half-open window, and everything else was taking a break, as if the whole neighborhood were holding its breath, no more planes or passersby calling out to each other as they left the bar down the road, no more buses or sirens or humming fridges, an eclipse. Lara was stretched out on her front, Cléo, straddling her buttocks, was massaging her painful trapezius muscles, Lara's mind hit a logjam of images, Cléo's hand on her shoulder blades, Cléo's hand along her sides, under her armpit, Lara saw the entire moment as a static cloud, the present writ large. Cléo barely rises, Lara rolls over, and then, from the tip of the toes to the palm of the hands, her breasts against hers, Cléo covers her, her hips against Lara's, who opens up and slides towards Cléo's sex.

That was the first time, she murmured. And Cléo, smiling: all the better. Then Lara: was it no big deal to her? Had there been many girls? Which one? Mélanie with the peroxide hair?

Your skin's an outrage, said Lara, her cheek resting in the hollow of Cléo's groin. Cléo's silence accentuated the emphasis of the words, but it didn't matter. What had she been doing all these years? What had she been doing with her body, her sex?

Cléo's legs were marked with bruises, shades of blue: Lara traced, with her finger, the hard skin of the rough heel, the thighs smelling of arnica, that bulge of the quadriceps, she restricted Cléo's movement, her knee slipped between the dancer's warm thighs, nose in her neck, breath taken away, the pleasure surged without a prelude, went right through her.

Cléo brought Lara tea in bed before leaving for class, bought her the rye-and-honey bread she was mad about, massaged her feet after her shift at the tearoom, laughed at Lara's imitations of Delphine. Cléo said, *As you like, it's all fine by me*, when Lara suggested a choice of two movies, two exhibitions.

Cléo, who'd just celebrated her twenty-seventh birthday,

seven years older than Lara, was a kid. Who got the giggles when she said the word "pussy." Who did silly dares: bet you she'd ask the baker for a "*braguette*"—trouser fly—instead of a baguette. Who was incapable of planning what she'd do that summer, it was "too far away." Who got undressed by throwing her clothes in a heap, her bedroom was a teenager's pigsty, grumbled Lara, as she tripped on a towel rolled in a ball, or a magazine.

It was cute, that way her roommate had of saying "*envoir*" instead of "*au revoir*," Ivan, a friend from the collective, had commented. Lara had rebuked him, mocking errors of speech, that was class contempt. As for her, she gently corrected the dancer, AU-RE-VOIR. And one didn't say "*ramener du café*" but rather "*rapporter*."

Cléo had vaguely mentioned that she'd grown up in a suburb east of Paris. When Lara had enquired about the "living conditions" of her parents, Cléo had guffawed: the word "suburb" had been said, so Lara picturing was tower blocks and drug dealers. The housing-project apartments in Fontenay were spacious and bright, her mother worked in a clothes store in Paris, her father, well, he'd struggled to find work after being made redundant, today he worked in the stockroom at Carrefour. Cléo admired her mother for always *smashing it*: you'd leave her store with a sweater, even if you'd not meant to buy a thing.

The dancer's fighting talk made Lara feel uncomfortable, she rolled her eyes, for pity's sake, no Bernard Tapie talk in *her* bed. As did that way Cléo had of planting herself in front of the full-length mirror in the sitting room, squaring up to herself as though to an enemy: *lazy big lump*.

Cléo's verbal violence swirled around, swooped down, sparing only Malko: that cameraman could just drop dead, doing close-ups of her breasts without warning her. Lucky that Malko was there to watch out for her. That presenter was a swine fit for slaughter, showering the dancers with compliments, then scoring them from one to ten in the TF1 cafeteria once he'd bedded them. But Malko had his eye on him.

Lara scoffed at the way Cléo revered the man Lara called "the boss"; Cléo had protested: he was a master. Not a boss. And furthermore, her parents worshipped that politico Tapie.

"You never told me that" became Lara's leitmotif, she wanted to know everything. For nothing to remain in the dark. Cléo hadn't done her *baccalauréat*. She read extracts of the Torah, admired its philosophy. Opium, the Saint Laurent perfume, made her nauseous. She'd never really had a serious love affair. She didn't hate making love with boys, she just found it really boring. She didn't have many memories of her adolescence. For her, being a body that danced was knowing to stop on the verge of pain, like on the verge of an orgasm. She defended the concept of a popular poetry: songs. Words, when they succeeded in moving us deeply, changed us.

Lara sometimes thought this: actually, Cléo's pretty smart— only to correct herself immediately: Cléo was more complex than she let on.

Lara shared her university dilemmas with Cléo: sociology, Anglo-Saxon literature, history, she couldn't decide for next year. Lara had no pressing desires. Except for Cléo. She drew her towards her, onto her, into her.

Everything had changed. Lara surveyed the men in the street, she'd never make love with a single one of them ever again. She was leaving them, the way you close the door of a holiday home that was comfy, yet too familiar.

She wondered: how should she announce this to the others? I'm in love with my roommate, I'm going out with Cléo. At the end of a meeting, to shut up a new arrival who'd called the collective "preachers," Lara had finally said it: I'm sleeping with one of Drucker's dancers, you should see her abs! One afternoon in April, Cléo had joined her at the end of a demonstration; at the café, Lara showed Cléo off, stroking the dancer's throat with her fingertips while still talking with her friends, intoxicated by their surreptitious glances.

T*here's something I want to tell you*, Cléo had begun, one Friday evening while preparing supper. She had paused, it wasn't urgent, then finally changed her mind: she was a bit tired, wanted an early night. Cléo had said nothing.

A few days later, sitting in their favorite restaurant in Belleville, Cléo had said it again: *I think I need to tell you something.*

Serious? Or really, really serious? Lara had asked, cheerily, her fear rising suddenly, like some crazy mercury in a thermometer: Cléo was about to reveal to her that she'd slept with the peroxide-blond dancer.

Back at the apartment, Lara had sat down in the kitchen, facing her roommate, anticipating the break-up, mustn't be in her arms when she'd announce to her that, sorry, but . . .

Well, here goes.

Cléo's parents weren't in what Lara called a "precarious" position. But they clung to their life, their work, as though to a favor granted them. Conversations around the table almost systematically ended with a *that's just the way it is*. They were preparing her for nothing ever to happen.

Saturday afternoons in winter, for Cléo, amounted to going round in circles on the Fontenay ice rink to the strains of Kim Wilde. The boys showed off by skating backwards, the girls watched them, spectators working at turning themselves into prey. On Saturday afternoons in spring, she and her friends hung around the stores in the Créteil Soleil mall, trying on everything and buying nothing. They nicked a little, it was pretty easy.

Only dancing, Stan's classes, had the power to shake up the ordinariness of a dreary life that just dragged on. There, she could invent herself.

One February day, at the youth and culture center, she'd been approached by a woman. Very stylish. Her mother's age, maybe a bit less. The woman that Cléo refused to name had *chosen* her. Why her? Because she was the youngest in the class, perhaps.

She'd had no reason not to believe in the existence of the Galatea Foundation. Why wouldn't a Galatea Foundation have existed? Awarding grants to the most deserving candidates. That woman had *taught* her beauty. She'd taken her to Paris. To grand restaurants, to antique dealers, to Guerlain, into Parisian bookstores, to watch movie classics. Her mother had met her; she, too, had been impressed.

Lara stopped Cléo: what was she talking about, a first lesbian affair? With an older woman? How old was Cléo?

Cléo was bombarded with fragmented images, summoning them up was exhausting her: the apartment smelt of damp. A street in Paris in the sixteenth arrondissement. The guys, those judges, no more than four or five of them, as many as there were girls. Girls who never said a word to each other during those *lunches*, no bonding between them. Zero chat. Every girl for herself. May the best girl win. What were they winning? Two or three banknotes. There were bedrooms all along the corridor.

But how old were you? Lara asked, again.

They were on the sagging sofa in the sitting room, through the window, the broad moon dominated the May night. Cléo, knees drawn up to chest, played with her bare toes.

She'd claimed not to have any childhood memories: now

she had a whole drawer of them, wide open to Lara, full of disjointed words, sullied words, night terrors, and shame.

After *that particular occasion*, she'd started having stomachaches every night. She had nothing to vomit. Everything was empty, of meaning, of words, she hadn't said no, she'd consented, but to what.

How old were you? Lara asked, again, the mercury soaring crazily up into her throat.

Cléo shook her head, it was of no importance.

Cléo had complied. Like those Lara spoke of with disdain, employees obeying the boss. She'd contaminated the others. At school, when they talked about what they'd do later on, they'd ended with a *mustn't dream*. Cléo had encouraged them to dream. To wish for all those things Cléo was sure had been the norm for Lara: doing a course at a dancing school, or in tennis, thinking of becoming an interpreter, a stylist . . .

Those girls had never come to find Cléo in the schoolyard *afterwards*. As if they'd all signed some pact.

What haunted her was not knowing. Whether Cléo had been the only girl for whom the lunches . . . Or whether, on the contrary, everything had gone the same way for each girl. Cléo could almost forget about those girls. But not about Betty. Not Betty at all.

Betty's mother needed money, Betty talked about money all the time. She'd managed to discover the meeting place. Cléo had done nothing. She'd listened to Betty selling herself. Boasting about her medals. Giving her phone number.

Cléo pushed Lara's hand away, she didn't deserve to be consoled.

How old were you, Cléo? Lara asked, again.

They had gone to bed in silence; Cléo, snuggled against Lara's back, had fallen asleep straight away.

Most people who met her thought Cléo was younger than Lara. The first time she'd seen her smile, Lara had thought Cléo had pretty little girl's teeth. Now, everything seemed to indicate that Cléo would be thirteen years old for all eternity, she was banging into that eternity's every dead angle.

L
ara was confronted with a revealed Cléo. A Cléo like a playing card for grown-ups, a simple jack who'd dreamt of being queen. Heads, victim, and tails, guilty.

How many accomplices had allowed this ninepin game to take place? The dance teacher at the youth and culture center, who'd seen that woman coming to pick up Cléo on several occasions without ever asking who she was; the doctors called to Cléo's bedside who didn't pose a single question that might have allowed her to speak out; Cléo's parents, never surprised at the gifts she brought home; the waitress who oversaw those "lunches." And who else?

Lara made herself the child-Cléo's advocate, she wanted to shower her with gentleness and forgiveness.

But all the same. How could she? Cléo knew exactly what would happen to the other girls. She'd *chosen* other girls, persuaded them. She'd alerted no one.

And she continued to protect the person she called "that woman," naively arguing that it was possible she'd known nothing of what took place at those lunches.

Lara considered all that made Cléo a sought-after dancer: her resilience to pain, her competitiveness, that capacity to execute exactly what she'd been asked. To reproduce gestures, feelings. Cléo performing, under the orders of a choreographer, a director, a chief cameraman. Cléo protected by a TV screen, concealed behind a mask of foundation and a smile painted on with a brush.

*

Just as she did with movies, Lara had decided: some feminist friends were organizing a weekly discussion group devoted to the victims of sexual violence, she knew a girl who worked on the prostitution of minors . . .

Cléo raised her voice: I don't want you talking about it with other people, I don't suffer from what was done to me, I suffer from what I didn't do, I'm a victim of nothing. She slammed the door, came back gentle and confused: she wanted to forget. No. She wanted to know.

Cléo exuded fear, pursued by five little letters: B E T T Y.

Cléo, whose smile and spangly bra were known to all of France, was a fugitive incapable of measuring the gravity of what she'd done because she wasn't conscious of the acts she herself had been subjected to. Lara reread Cléo in the light of what she'd just learnt, she'd ceased to be a stranger, she lay there, innards revealed, offered up to all interpretations. Words cut into the delightful haziness of their budding relationship, each one concealing new traps. If Lara praised the trust among members of the collective, Cléo immediately closed up: of course, *now*, Lara wouldn't trust *her* anymore.

If Lara was surprised to learn that Cléo refused to lower her fee for a young choreographer, the dancer became bitter: she wasn't enough of an artist, was too venal—was that the message? This latent suffering resurfaced every other minute, that of a former girl to whom adults had taught the lonesomeness of betrayal.

One evening in spring, returning from a gala in the provinces, Cléo had joined them in the kitchen. The collective's meeting was drawing to a close in a smoky hubbub, the tract they'd just written ending with: "Let's drop job-sharing for joy-sharing! We're not asking for sugar-coated exploitation or poverty!"

Just as one pushes a shy child to recite a poem in front of guests, Lara encouraged Cléo to tell them about her working life: the badly paid—if paid at all—rehearsals, the TV recordings until midnight with no overtime pay, the humiliations, the rivalry at auditions . . . Cléo toned it down: when you're part of a show, you're not going to count the hours. The cruelty of auditions, yes, of course, but not everyone could be a dancer, it was the art of excellence.

Lara became annoyed: one had to see bigger than just one's own case, see thing more politically. A young guy entered the ring to fight with gusto for an already partisan audience: surely Cléo wasn't going to claim that it was a choice, that she liked working in mass entertainment? For Drucker, for fuck's sake! She couldn't not question what she was a part of!

Yes, she could. That's what she liked doing, entertaining. And . . . how was dancing on the Théâtre de la Ville stage more respectable than on a set for TV? What was their criterion for deciding that a show was alienating? Because it was watched by millions of TV viewers? Malko had turned dance into a popular art. Where was the harm in that?

Cléo and the other dancers on set were "neighborhood dancers." Accessible. In Malko's company there was an Asian girl, two dancers of Arab origin, a black girl, and while Cléo herself was athletic, two other dancers were pretty frail. Maybe Cléo made kids want to dance who'd never dare go to the Palais Garnier? Who'd had their first lesson in a youth and culture center, like her?

Cléo was right, Lara agreed, TV could broadcast good shows, not just revues of naked girls, like on New Year's Eve.

What was wrong with revues? asked Cléo, turning to Lara. The nudity?

Before Lara could even reply, a girl retorted: surely Cléo wasn't going to defend *that sort* of dancer? Feathers, G-strings, and all that? Revues were tacky things aimed at frustrated schmucks who came to jerk off over women they couldn't even touch. These women harmed feminism!

They all went quiet, stunned by the turn the discussion was taking, and by Cléo, who usually stayed in the background. Standing, feet slightly apart, she tightened the elastic of her ponytail, Okay, so for them, a show was judged based on the social origins of its spectators, "schmucks?" Well, her parents were schmucks. And she was one, too.

And "that sort" of dancer? Those at the Lido were mainly ballet dancers who'd grown too tall to join a classical company. At the Moulin Rouge, the cancan demanded learning a technique passed on since the turn of the twentieth century. None of this "sort" of girls did what the collective called a "shit job." As for feminism . . . The girls in the collective disguised themselves as men to be taken seriously, whereas she, Cléo, disguised herself as a woman on Drucker's show.

Lara, say something, the debate's lost its way, begged a young man, twirling around the table on socked tiptoes, arms crowning head in a caricature of ballet.

You're angry? a girl asked Cléo. No, no problem, she was thick-skinned.

The following morning, Lara had woken up to find a day-old message on the answering machine from Delphine.

Lara was moaning to a Cléo in pajamas drinking tea: Delphine was going to force them to wear a pseudo-American-style uniform. But no doubt Cléo would find it very becoming, having given a whole speech last night on the subversive side of diamanté G-strings . . .

You don't like it when I say what I think, you don't like what I think, you don't like the way I speak, whispered the dancer, as if to herself, an observation.

What you like is to watch me from afar. Yesterday evening, you watched me from afar.

Did Lara remember that day, in the café, when she'd explained to Cléo how the collective stuck together in demonstrations, each keeping an eye on one another, making sure they were all safe?

Yesterday, Lara hadn't stood up for her.

Lara received her letter of dismissal the following Monday. Delphine hadn't even had the guts to tell her to her face. She didn't care, she'd find something else. As for Cléo, she was about to rejoin Malko's troupe for a series of galas in the provinces.

They phoned each other every day, since they couldn't see each other, short, trivial conversations; when she hung up,

Lara felt as sad as a child after Christmas. They got together on the weekends, Lara slipping into the dancer's bed the way one drifts off after a sleepless night, reassured by Cléo's thighs gripping her hips, briefly soothed by her undiminished pleasure.

The terms chosen by Lara to inform Cléo of her decision to break up seemed lifted from a redundancy-scheme announcement; she feared the dancer would protest, but she did nothing of the sort. It was funny, Cléo simply pointed out to her, that when they'd met, it had been Lara serving and Cléo being served. She'd said nothing more, giving Lara to understand that very swiftly, between them, the roles had been reversed. She returned the key to her without seeming affected by their parting, nodded when Lara told her that not being desperate to remain a couple was also a political act.

A while later, Lara found a little square of paper between the pages of a book; when they'd been in love, Cléo would leave little notes everywhere for Lara, on the kitchen table, under the pillow, taped to the shampoo bottle in the bathroom.

In her spiky handwriting, Cléo had written: *With you, I learn so much.*

She saw the dancer again once, in autumn 1999—Cléo had forgotten a sweater in her room—and then heard nothing for twenty years.

■ ■ ■

Lara has kept all of Cléo's little notes in a book, along with that front page of *Le Parisien* from March 1999, the photo of a demonstration with the finest of the collective's banners at its head: "We're not against the aged, we're against what ages them."

She often lets weeks go by before answering emails, a way of reasserting the right to time, of removing the bossy suddenness of these messages, which loom up rather than arrive. The one from this adrien@superbox.fr, with *CLÉO* as its subject, begins thus: I know that my wife and you were very close . . .

Cléo, soon to be fifty, is married to an Adrien. If it doesn't hurt, you just haven't disturbed anything.

6

That smugness of day planners when you no longer have any use for them, flaunting the blankness of their pages. Since she's been retired, it's out of sheer habit that Claude still jots down in hers: Doctor 2 P.M. Read *Le Monde* article. Buy tomatoes with mozzarella.

And, written on the November 19 page, every year: "Send birthday email to Cléo." A task made impossible on this November 19, 2019, due to a computer screen refusing to show anything but a disturbing expanse of turquoise.

When she called her son for help, Nico grumbled that not everyone was retired, he couldn't just leave his work the moment his mother was in a digital panic, he'd pop by that evening.

Nico speaks to her with the weariness of a teacher worn out by an obtuse pupil's mediocrity, he's told her a thousand times: don't touch a thing if the computer malfunctions. At what moment does a son turn into a suspicious father one lies to? Claude thought it best not to mention her frantic stabbing at the keyboard.

Without taking his eyes off the screen, Nico starts on his ritual round of "you coulds": you could go on hikes for the over-fifties, you could learn to draw, try pottery, calisthenics.

On Claude's kitchen table, he regularly leaves health magazines, an anti-stress coloring book, St. John's wort capsules, great against depression and not addictive. So many offerings for days he seems to fear will swallow her up. The woman who is the focus of this attentiveness bears no resemblance to Claude. At what moment does a son lose sight of the woman who has been his mother, and replace her with a fictional figure: jam-making granny, cart-pushing old dear, content to lead a slower life.

Whenever Claude mentions the years spent squeezing time to get extra minutes out of it, her past as a dresser at Diamantelles, Nico gets annoyed: forty-five years of playing the maid, that's quite enough, now she can make the most of her time.

Maid?

Being a dresser is doing many jobs at once, but not that of a maid: she was the laundress with all the washing and ironing to do, not to mention dousing the dancers' sixty G-strings in antibacterial spray every day. She became an emergency worker, capable, in a thirty-second scene change, of restitching a torn Lycra crotch.

She'd turned into a psychologist, assuming a false serenity to rush to the aid of those calling for her, CLAUUUDE, half an hour before curtain-up.

She'd had the great good fortune of sharing her life with so many people with rare skills: embroiderers, feather experts, footwear specialists . . . Without forgetting her girls, of course.

Her son listens to her with a patience that makes Claude feel like she's no longer all there. No doubt his shrink has advised him to "distance himself from his mother's symptoms."

Claude would sooner have the young man's annoyance when he catches her repeating herself, his speed at crying out: "Mom, you've already said that." His anxiousness to highlight her weakness to her moves her deeply. Nico is still her frightened child, a man terrified by the impending decline, and death, of his mom: *You've already said that.*

Nico switches the computer off, and back on, one more

time, it doesn't work; anyway, Claude doesn't really *need* her emails.

She points at the diary, it's Cléo's birthday. She really would have liked to send her an email today, she ventures, vaguely ashamed at allowing the persistence of her desires to show, like a breach in the serenity of her retirement. Cléo's last message, last week, concerns her a little . . .

That gentle, soothing way her son speaks to her: It's nice of her. Nevertheless, this pseudo-friendship with Cléo, which his mother fears breaking, rests on a twenty-year-old feeling of guilt. How much longer is she going to keep on about that business, snaps Nico. At the time, Claude did what any divorcee with a child would have done: she sought to keep her job. So Cléo, the cabaret militant, can keep her reproaches.

Cléo has never remotely reproached her, stammers Claude. Exactly.

Nico glances at his mobile phone; the allotted time for his visit is over, and he's keen to wrap up, his mother's old age is making him moody and late. Claude can just send a normal birthday card to her Cléo. *End of discussion.*

Claude closes the door on her son. On the table in the sitting room, the black digital box remains placidly silent. Once, to Nico, who was forever throwing the word *"retraitée"*— retiree—at her, she'd read out the dictionary definition of the noun *"retraite"*—retirement. The final definition was that of a "retreat": withdrawal of an army that cannot stand its ground.

Claude had "withdrawn."

In the mirror, the woman crying makes her smile, a stubborn old-young woman, the mother of around a hundred girls, including the one who would be celebrating her forty-eighth birthday today: Cléo.

...

H er girls. That racket they made as they arrived at their dressing rooms at 5 P.M., calling out to each other in Polish, Russian, English—language the only distinguishing feature among those who, on the attendance board, were all anonymously called "mademoiselle," whether married or not.

Her girls. Similar from year to year. Those who, victims of a strap snapping just once, then fretted every night, as if it were a curse forever hanging over them.

Those who, with makeup removed, looked sick, anemically pale. Those who winced when Claude helped them into their heels, hiding a painful ankle for fear of being replaced. Those on opiates, their eyes glazed and mouths dry. Those with flushed cheeks, a side-effect of cortisone. Those who complained of a hangover every Monday. Those who gave her a box of marrons glacés at New Year, then tucked into them throughout the fitting. Those who lost—and then, in a childish panic, searched everywhere for—the woolen shawl they wrapped around their hips in rehearsals, a security blanket. Those who, in the wings, kept their headphones on until the last minute, humming to a hit nothing like the music coming from the auditorium. Those who held out their arms to Claude for her to slip on the support, that iron heart onto which the traditional indigo and gold pheasant feathers were attached. Those who boasted of having everything planned, they knew at *exactly* what age they would quit. Those who obsessed over some detail, using a skillful blend of foundations to hide a scar, a birthmark, like Cléo. Those who battled the two extra centimeters on their waist, just before their period, with diuretics. Those who were all aquiver when they knew a friend was in the audience and tried to stand out from the others by some detail, a hat worn lower. Those who spiced up the show by doing dares with another dancer, fifty francs that they'd stick their tongues out at the spectators during the "Sexy Kitten" scene. Those for whom it was the last performance, the end of a contract, when they were hugged, they looked upwards, index finger placed under bottom lid so as not to smudge the eyeliner, their tears powdered with a rosy sheen. Those who took photos of rehearsals for a friend, a brother in hospital, they never uttered those letters, HIV. Those who cheated by downing a liter-and-a-half of water before the weekly weigh-in, having lost too much weight. Those with a whiff of camphor and menthol, that salve applied to inflamed tendons. Those who didn't respond to the stage call, whom Claude found in a daze, sitting cross-legged on the gray linoleum of the dressing rooms, clutching a piece of paper, the doctor recommended that they take several months off. Those who pined for a fiancé left behind in Riga, those who'd just split up with a guy who'd insisted that they do *something other than that*. Those who worried about the first signs of cellulite and wore two pairs of tights, nude under fishnet. Those who, for ten years, had eaten but one meal a day, and recited a brownie recipe with passion. Those with arms crossed over breasts as soon as they encountered a stagehand in the wings. The new girls, unaccustomed to the sheer size of their headdress, preceded by the rustle of feathers crushed against the walls. The French girls, who benefited from a long-term contract. The others, who crossed Europe, from one cabaret to another, Russians, Romanians, afraid of being fired and losing their residency permit.

All of them, who'd "always dreamt of dancing" on this stage. Whose names weren't even mentioned in the programs, although none of these statistics were omitted: two million rhinestones, two hundred kilos of ostrich feathers, five kilos of petticoats for the French-cancan outfit, forty-five technicians.

Girls held to a contractual smile on stage, ranked in a strict hierarchy: at the bottom of the ladder, the "nude models," then the "dressed girls" and, among them, the aristocracy of the soloists, of whom the "*meneuse de revue*" was the shining star.

Bird-girls arranged in a fan of red and gold feathers, rows of long, creamy thighs reflected in two angled mirrors at the back of the stage.

All the girls, who went from a rehearsal to two shows a night, at 9 P.M. and 11:30 P.M., six days out of seven, and with no end-of-year bonus, public holidays, or lieu days. Fifty hours a week. All the girls paid less than the waiters at the establishment's "high-class" restaurant. Only on Christmas Day, New Year's Day, and May 1 was the pay doubled. All the girls dressed in blue, white, and red in the final scene, laced corsets and petticoats swishing over ankle boots to evoke the French Revolution, the grand finale.

All the girls who, as soon as they came off stage, extricated themselves from their costumes, which they left piled in a heap on the floor, for the dressers.

Returning to their dressing rooms, clutching their pumps, catching their breath, grousing about the girl beside them who'd almost brought them all down, bursting out laughing at the mention of a blunder, starving or nauseous, or both at once, some of them hugging her vigorously: OH MY CLAUDE, you saved my life yet again this evening!

Claude heard them moving off, and moaning: the water in

the shower's freezing / there's no more shower gel / who's got a tampon?

Arms loaded with damaged spangly stuff, rubbed satins, Claude went down to the lower basement, where the work-rooms were. Four Anglepoise lamps marked out her sewing table; along the walls, mobile dressing rooms were lined up in order of urgency, crimson corset-dresses, beaded mercerized cottons, crêpe-de-Chine veils, black gloves, and tiaras, all wait-ing to be examined.

Once she'd noted everything down, Claude would close the door as gently as if it were that of a child's bedroom.

The boss at Diamantelles had declared, to a journalist inter-viewing him, that the dancers at his establishment were like Formula One cars. If you wanted the vehicle to set off again as soon as possible, you had to surround it with a suitable team, expert at changing tires.

They had all learnt to be that, suitable. Dressers, light and sound engineers, stagehands: on arrival, they learnt the intri-cate choreography in the wings, which no incident or unfore-seen event must slow down.

It's that very atmosphere that Claude misses, now that she's retired. The challenge. Standing to one side, invisible, in the "quick-change dressing rooms," that airlock where the dressers undressed and redressed the dancers ten times per show, timed by the stage manager, forty-five seconds before the next scene. Ten times forty-five seconds of panting and sweat, of overexcited whispering drowned by the oompahs of the pre-recorded music blaring from the set. Claude bent down to crotch level to help them off with their G-strings, and, with one hand, repositioned a breast in an underwired bra. She sprinkled talc on an armpit irritated by the sequined fabric, dabbed a sweaty forehead with a towelette, handed a bottle of water to a breathless girl. To Claude, these moments seemed to give her a sharpness that was lost as soon as the ritual was over. She spotted everything: the crooked seam of a stocking, the tilting of a tiara, the loosened curls of a hairpiece, a damaged feather, a strip of rhinestones coming apart at the groin, the tense expression of an exhausted dancer.

When she met them for the first time, Claude asked them: what do you prefer for costume changes? Your back to me, or facing me?

They stared wide-eyed, unaccustomed to having a say in the matter.

The modesty of certain dancers was preserved in this one-on-one in the dark, when Claude was so close to them that she forgot their names.

To those whose abdomen tightened when Claude brushed against their inner thigh, Claude suggested that they keep their backs to her.

Claude knew all about them. All about their tall, panting bodies, their pains, a corn, tendonitis, their periods, all about their odd habits: this one stored her Thermos flask in the right-hand recess of a shelf, another covered her can of cola with tin-foil to keep it fizzy, taking a gulp between costume changes. These "racing cars" submitted to her scrutiny, they sought Claude's approval, her green light: they could hit the stage. Off you go!

In Claude's planner from 1999, the year they'd met, Cléo was merely numbers and colors: 1m 73 cm. 59 kg. 87/60/86. 28 years old. Red hair. Hazel eyes. Despite her size, average for a revue dancer, the new girl was highly regarded by the management. Cléo learnt fast and moved seamlessly from one dance style to another, a must for TV dancers.

On the day a soloist, an Australian girl, injured herself in rehearsal, it was only natural that Cléo was immediately picked to replace her, learning the steps at 5 P.M. to dance them at 8 P.M. The following week, she was promoted to being a "swing" dancer, an exhausting honor meaning she would now have to know several routines to be ready to replace any eventual absentees. The "swing" girl was always a concern for Claude; adapting one girl's costume for a different girl at the last minute meant finding "tricks." With pins clamped between lips and measuring tape around neck, Claude rummaged through PVC boxes full of swatches of fabric and reels of thread in every color: the Australian had the slender arms of a ballerina, but Cléo would need a bolero to conceal her triceps and deltoids. And would have to wear a headdress of tall garnet feathers to distract from the six centimeters she had less than Susanna, another injured dancer.

When Claude delivered the dancers' costumes to them, in their dressing rooms before the show, she'd hear Cléo passing on her "tricks" to the youngest girls, the best way to roll tights at the waist and secure them with the G-string elastic; or rec-ommending a foreign movie they really *must* see undubbed; or offering to help another girl cover her back in foundation; or giving her phone number to a twenty-year-old Russian girl who knew no one in Paris.

She'd even offered Claude, who was short of a babysitter, to go and collect Nico at school at 5 P.M.: Cléo was like those plump little ducks that were so eager to please, the "Junior Woodchucks" in her son's comics.

An adorable Junior Woodchuck, but with a quick tongue as unexpected as it was amusing, like the day when, to a lighting engineer complaining about her muscles—side lighting empha-sized her quadriceps—Cléo had retorted that she wasn't twelve years old, and if he liked little girls, he should look elsewhere.

Cléo, who preferred Claude to undress her from behind, approached everything head-on: she had no ambition whatso-ever to be a soloist, her "swing" position suited her fine. Being the double of the indisposed. Did she miss TV? Not really. Thanks to close-ups, one ended up becoming a well-known face, being hailed in the street. Or a famous butt, more like.

Claude listened to her flitting from one subject to another during fittings: had Claude read, the day before, the review of their show in such-and-such a newspaper? Not even under the heading "Shows," but rather "Entertainment"! And not one sentence on the dancers. Nothing on the costumes. Only "A must-see if you're into grandstanding" by way of a com-pliment. On the "Shows" page, there was praise for the "con-temporary cruelty" of a Belgian choreographer. Cléo had seen it, that ballet; if there was any cruelty, it was that of the cho-reographer towards his dancers: they seemed to be enduring their nudity, crouching under wan spotlights that accentuated their slightest flaws. Cléo had felt for them *right there*, her fin-ger pointing at her heart. If she'd understood correctly, there was the "groundbreaking" nudity lauded by middle-class spectators, and that in revues, reserved for hicks bused in from the sticks. Sheer class contempt.

Cléo had waited a few weeks before risking more personal subjects: did Claude have a boyfriend, or perhaps . . . a girl-friend? For Cléo, it wasn't easy being a lesbian in the dance world, she was suspected of ogling the girls in the showers. Some girls insinuated that Cléo owed her position to sleeping with the female director. Or then it was the technicians, whis-pering salacious remarks about a dancer to her, sure she'd appreciate them.

Cléo had been single since Lara. When she said that name, the final "a" was just a sigh, something worn out.

Before Lara, she'd been just a rough sketch of a girl. Lara was a fighter, she trampled over certainties, and Cléo wasn't used to that at the time. She'd understood everything, but too late. The word "split" was accurate: she'd been torn apart. But no one, least of all a girl like Lara, would have remained cou-pled up with a doormat.

When Cléo had left, Claude's feeling of unease had endured, at having witnessed the dancer's harshness when speaking of herself.

Three months after her arrival, Cléo told Claude about her concern for Jody, an English girl from Leeds. The scene called "Kitten on a Hot Roof" showed a feline silhouette swinging five meters above the audience, before a shower of golden glitter revealed the young girl clad in a tabby bodysuit with a long, fluffy tail, gripping a giant chandelier with her thighs. Jody had asked to be secured with a rope attached to her back: she wasn't an acrobat. The management had refused, deeming her to be perfectly safe.

Claude tempered Cléo's outrage: you had to believe them. It was hardly in their interest for any accident to happen.

Are you kidding, Claude? It was obvious. The management had done the sums: lights to be modified, costume to be adapted, it was an extra half-day's work to be paid for. Too much expense for a dancer.

Awkward at being made to take sides, to question the integrity of those for whom she was proud to have worked for a quarter of a century, Claude had stammered that, this evening, she'd watch the scene carefully.

C laude had noticed that, for a while, at rehearsals, the ballet mistress seemed never to miss Cléo's slightest lapses, reprimanding her for a chin held too high, for hands placed too low on the hips. The rumor was going around that Cléo's contract wouldn't be renewed. Claude had advised her to avoid getting involved in the management's business.

Cléo, topless in a red tulle petal-skirt and sports socks, had turned around sharply: avoid? As in, shut her mouth? Was that Claude's advice? Great. No wonder the union here had remained undercover until 1995. At least six dancers agreed with her about Jody. Not to mention the technicians, who were just finalizing a petition. Cléo had read it; she'd soon be circulating it, including to Claude, obviously.

In twenty-five years, Claude had witnessed slammed doors, raised voices, and tears. Waiters "replaced" or dancers "thanked": the turnover at the company was more than thirty percent a year, upheavals Claude kept her distance from, waiting for them to fade away. It was the business of the second floor, of a boss who gave her chocolates at Easter and asked after Nico. But these rumblings kept getting louder. Cléo wasn't the only one to echo them. A "nude" girl had pinned up her pay slip in the entrance of the establishment: even the few boys in the show were better paid than her. A stagehand had just been refused a seniority bonus. And Jody was still swinging up in the air, the iron branches of the chandelier leaving their dark-red imprint on the inside of her thighs. After every performance, the English girl slathered them with a soothing cream; to think she had vertigo and, as a kid, dodged mountain hikes! she quipped.

As for Cléo, she seemed to have followed Claude's advice: she kept quiet, an exemplary and versatile "swing" girl, from Egyptian belly dancer to tricolored *cancaneuse*, sporting a plume or a top hat, who put up with too-tight shoes and too-short costume changes.

On November 19, 1999, Claude gave Cléo, for her birthday, a sailor top like those the Junior Wood-chucks wore.

The dancer thanked her, with a burst of laughter, and left the workshop, but then tapped on the door again, oops, she'd almost forgotten to leave this: the petition for signing.

That sheet of paper encroached even on Claude's nights: signing it would jeopardize her position, she had a child to support, rent to pay. Signing it would be showing solidarity with "her girls." Signing it would be pointless, Claude was just a small cog in the company, not even the chief dresser.

In the morning, tiredness made her bleary-eyed, she had to make two attempts at threading a needle: few dressers worked beyond sixty, the threat of a life devoid of crises, of the dancers' puffing and panting, the fear of that made her dizzy. Claude curled up in search of sleep, chasing Cléo from her mind.

When writing her orders, sitting at her desk, Claude could just see a corner of the photocopied document, getting covered, day by day, in invoices and fabric samples.

Cléo came to the workshop about a troublesome fastener, a mending job, she'd not asked her a thing.

New Year's Eve was approaching, and Claude was worried about the "millennium bug," the secretaries talked of nothing else. Cléo was young, she was part of this new world of screens, whereas Claude, she was only comfortable with her registers—

at least her index cards wouldn't be swallowed up by this world to come!

Arms raised, while Claude replaced the corset's sharp hook with a snap-fastener, the dancer didn't respond.

She got dressed again, and then, with her fingertips, extricated the A4 sheet of paper from a pile of shimmery fabrics. She calmly folded the petition and slipped it into her sports bag, in front of Claude, and then, at the door:

Don't kid yourself, Claude, you totally belong to the new world, and I don't.

Cléo had been right. The end of the world hadn't occurred on the eve of the year 2000 but on the following day, and the spectators hadn't noticed a thing, those Japanese businessmen, those couples who'd traveled from Hamburg or Poitiers. Hadn't noticed the three dancers missing from the "Ça C'est Paris" scene, dismissed that very morning, without warning. All three had circulated the petition. Cléo's contract ended in January, it wasn't renewed. She didn't come to tell Claude about it. The new "swing" girl was twenty, and thrilled to have passed the audition, standing perfectly still while Claude measured her, barely breathing.

In November 2000, Claude sent a birthday card to Cléo.

Claude had considered adding a P.S. to her wishes, "Good news, two technicians finally got their seniority bonus," but, in the end, didn't.

In 2002, for the first time since the opening of the establishment, a small group of Lido dancers greeted spectators on the pavement outside, behind a banner decrying their working conditions.

In 2013, the Crazy Horse dancers refused to go on stage for two consecutive nights, to make their demands heard.

In 2014, to the eighty Diamantelles employees gathered in the auditorium one late afternoon in April, the director presented a pleasant young man who had graduated from a London business school.

Dressed in dark-red chinos and a sky-blue polo shirt, he announced that the word "employee" would no longer be used, too condescending: from now on, they would form a team. His immaculate sneakers appeared never to have touched pavement.

It was time for Diamantelles to quit its "comfort zone" and move towards a more "dynamic" show, featuring more scenes, but shorter ones. For example, in the one named "French Revolution," fifteen girls would suffice, would dance more. Premiums were planned for the more acrobatic numbers, the risk factor would be taken into account. Tradition? It would be respected, with feathers, sequins, the whole shebang, but revamped. The objective: send the sexy level sky high. He used the word "flexibility" several times: the flexibility of working hours, flexibility in the new types of contracts. Performers weren't state employees! To Claude, he gave a large book with a leather cover that she didn't dare use, neither for logging orders nor anything else.

The young man's assistant received her one morning in a small office on the second floor. The young girl was wearing a dark T-shirt, its underarms whitened by deodorant. Claude had almost recommended an appropriate stain-remover to her; instead, she'd listened to her firing her, nodding her head like one of those bobbing dogs in the back window of a car. Once she'd finished her spiel, the young girl got up, and, for a few moments, they faced each other, neither knowing what to do or say: should one say thank you for having been "thanked," wish each other all the best, or just a nice day?

For the last time, that evening, Claude knelt at the feet of the girls who would learn the following day that, owing to "creative changes," their contract would be terminated in ninety days' time.

That year, her birthday card for Cléo had proved too small, so Claude had attached half an A4 sheet of paper.

"Thanked." Doubtless because of her bad hands: she'd been diagnosed with polyarthritis. They'd better not count on Claude attending the opening of the new show!

A stand that was too little, too late, when she'd been among those who'd politely held open the door to this new world, pretending not to notice its discreet progress as the years went by. Being indignant in 2014 about the echo of a rumbling first detected in 1999.

Cléo probably didn't understand the meaning of that second card, sent by Claude the very next day, with just three words on it: I'm sorry, Cléo.

The reply reached her three months later, a handwritten letter, in which childish crossings-out contrasted with the almost didactic content: for Claude to apologize to her, Cléo would have needed to have made some complaint. Maybe it was better to forget? Actually, had Claude read that Milan Kundera novel in which Cléo had found this: "Everything will be forgotten and nothing will be redressed"? Cléo proposed forgetting, but Claude herself dreaded forgetting: not a day went by without her confronting lapses in her memory, a word escaping her, a pair of keys mislaid . . .

The oldest memories, on the contrary, came back to her with precision: those summer nights, when Claude's father hoisted her onto the low wall in the garden. And then her hands, splayed in the dusk as though in dark water, until she even felt the beam of a rising moon slip through her fingers.

C laude had finally opted for email: paper betrayed, revealed the shaking of her stiff hand too much. The computer smoothed out time. Thanks to it, Cléo still addressed her former dresser, not that lady with the deformed fingers. Claude, on the other hand, addressed that brusque and helpful girl with the powerful thighs, who'd taught her that she was a coward.

With only a few arrondissements separating them, Cléo and Claude kept up a regular rhythm of exchanges. The ex-dancer had gotten married to . . . a man. She'd informed Claude of it by adding a "What the fuck?!" to the official announcement.

She told Claude about her adolescent daughter, who judged Cléo's time at Diamantelles harshly, their shows "perpetuated patriarchal norms." Cléo followed the expression with a series of ellipses. If that was true, Claude and Cléo would have contributed to harming hundreds of women, without even suspecting it.

There'd been talk of meeting up on several occasions, without it happening.

■ ■ ■

And today, for the first time since they met, Cléo, forty-eight years old, won't receive her virtual birthday card.

When Claude finally manages to get reconnected the

following day, all the messages in her inbox have been erased. She writes the following to Junior Woodchuck: a computer has seen fit to erase their *History*, isn't that a wonderful birthday present, starting all over again?

7

SURNAME: *if you don't wish to answer this question, go to the next one.

FIRST NAME: *if you don't wish to answer this question, go to the next one.

Anton moves the computer's cursor back and forth across the page, undecided.

IN WHAT WAY DO YOU THINK YOUR TESTIMONY COULD HELP US?

The cursor hovering on the page, like the needle of scales that can't gauge the weight of Anton's decision. In his inbox, an email from his aunt, subject: Wednesday?

■ ■ ■

Until very recently, Anton only saw her at birthdays, Christmas and Easter. His aunt with the broad thighs, and the bronze complexion she didn't rosy up with blush, so unlike the other women of the family, who were uniformly refashioned, from their eyebrows to the padded bras showing through their T-shirts. His aunt with the ample body, present at every family reunion but absent from the most banal conversations. His aunt, more childish than a child, who sometimes made him feel as if she'd robbed him of his age. While Anton was congratulated for his achievements, his aunt stood out for what she didn't achieve, in a family that valued motherhood and appearances above all else: for her, there was neither a child, nor a diet, nor a hairdresser, no more than there was a career plan. She'd been a sales assistant at a florist's, receptionist at a veterinary clinic, had signed up for correspondence courses in psychology and social sciences. Each episode ending without anyone knowing who'd chosen to end it, her or an employer tired of her absences. Because she "caught everything": bugs, viruses, and lumbagos.

When Anton was a child, the family would gather for a week in August at a rental property beside a lake; she'd scoop up the car keys as if they were dice in a game and disappear for the whole day. At dinnertime, she was back and could be heard opening the fridge, cutting a slice of bread, and then, declining the invitation to join the family around the table, she'd go up to her room, clutching a plate of buttered bread. When Anton needed the bathroom in the middle of the night, he'd find her curled up on the sofa, reading, with a pot of tea at her feet. Just as he was slowly extricating himself from childhood, his aunt was floating between adolescence and maturity.

Seven years ago, when she was forty, his aunt had revived hope: she'd found herself "someone!" If she and this Robin got on with it pronto, she still stood a small chance of becoming pregnant. Then, seeing nothing happening, the family had praised Robin's selflessness: staying with a woman who didn't provide him with a child, didn't earn, or barely earned, a living, and didn't "groom" herself, that really was proof of love.

But Robin dismissed such praise: he saw enough of kids at school, where he was an educational adviser. And he was proud of his partner being a volunteer representative of the Animalêtre-Île-de-France association on Facebook, responding to messages at all hours.

His aunt: the glaring rip in a dress, the persistent stain. That of a *story*. All families were woven with stories, which were perpetuated by a chorus of lives. Those sedimentary stories cemented the clan more securely than births and birthdays, those evocations of that day when, that time when . . .

But Anton's family was woven with a *story* that was never evoked. Not because it had been forgotten, but because everyone knew it. The *story* was part of the furniture, everyone knew not to bang into it. A *story* riddled with awkward silences, of which his aunt was the main actress, even if the role she played in it was hazy, almost erased.

Anton knew its prologue and its ending: his aunt, a dark-haired little girl with nut-brown skin had modestly started ballet classes at a youth and culture center, then, as an adolescent, thanks to hard work, had won two bronze medals in different competitions. Thirty years on, the family still couldn't believe it: one morning, the year she was eighteen, she'd announced that it was all over, both the dancing and the suited forty-something fiancé invited to every Sunday lunch.

All that effort, just to end up like that. The "like that" referred to a body on strike that Anton, as a child, would surreptitiously look at, trying to detect traces of the dancer she'd once been: that way of positioning the feet turned out. The slenderness of the wrists contrasting with the plump upper arms. That smooth way she had of moving around, like gliding.

There was something obscene about scrutinizing his aunt like this, something cruel in wanting to stick a white tutu on this sizeable body, relieving her of the light-collared blouses and short skirts she wore all year round. Something traitorous, too, in imitating the adults and, like them, prefacing his aunt's name with a concerned sigh. When Anton found her so beautiful. But belonging to a family meant being loyal to the functioning of a clan, perpetuating what was.

Until October 13, 2019.

Anton's birthday dinner was an event not one member of his family missed. They all came to celebrate the one they dubbed "the little prince." They ruffled his hair, as if still not used to his extreme blondness; his mother had worried that he'd "darken" as he grew up, but no such thing had occurred, fortunately! Every birthday was an occasion to tell the story of that first time they'd seen baby Anton: but who did he look like? Certainly not his parents, or his uncles, who were dark, eyes and all! It felt to Anton as if they were all spectators of his life, like staying for both screenings of a movie one never tires of watching. Noisy and loving spectators gathered together, on this October evening, to celebrate his fourteenth birthday.

His grandmother and mother bustled back and forth, their cheeks crimson, slipping an extra piece of meat onto his plate, here you go, it's well done, just as you like it. As for Anton, he was holding forth. What he'd read, what he'd seen, what he was working on at school: the way the press had reported on two similar stories, ten years apart. In 2005, a former tennis player had revealed that, at fourteen, she'd been the victim of sexual abuse by her forty-something coach, and the story hadn't caused much of a stir. Today, the media would have devoted several pages to it, like it had for that actress in her thirties who accused a director of controlling behavior and sexual abuse; he'd given her her first part at the age of twelve, and in an interview, gave as an excuse the passion she'd inspired in him.

The history teacher described the MeToo phenomenon as revolution rather than evolution. Anton's sister, Dafina, mocked his enthusiasm: help! her little brother was a feminist!

Their grandmother had shaken her head, and suggested they move on to dessert, and to *something else.*

Then a voice had piped up, a voice like rain, timid and tepid. His aunt had turned towards him, like a lost tourist asking the way. Excuse me, but . . .

How could you know whether a story was "MeToo?" Were there criteria?

His aunt consulted Anton as though he were some eminent expert; the collar of her white blouse stood out, like two stiff wings, on her navy sweater. She pronounced MeToo as *"Mitou,"* as though calling a kitten. The directness of her voice belied the softness of her tilted face, as his aunt with the sea-green eyes went through her questions:

If the director stated that he was in love with the actress, was it still *Mitou?*

If he'd contributed to her career? *Mitou?*

What did he say about it, the teacher?

And the young ones, at school?

Everyone around the table rigid, seemingly waiting for Anton to decide to move on to *something else.*

Something was hovering, something threatening, and each one of them guarded against it: Robin had entwined his fingers around his aunt's. His father was clearing his throat, like before a speech. A cousin was absorbed in the contemplation of wax stains on the tablecloth. An uncle had gotten up to go and smoke at the window, as if the meal were over.

Before Anton could even reply, voices, all these voices, rose up, hurriedly smoothing out the blue of a horizon disrupted by the flight of a bird with small white wings.

These women had no modesty / it was important, modesty

/ all this, just an offloading of revelations / everything got mixed up, these days / it was tragic for the *real* victims / it was getting ridiculous, these complaints lodged over the slightest thing.

The orchestra of voices went quiet. The rain had stopped.

With the candles barely blown out, Robin had looked at his watch, said thanks for the dinner, see you at Christmas. He'd taken his leave of the whole table with a wave; to Anton, he held out his hand. When his aunt leant towards Anton to kiss him, he muttered *later*. We'll talk about it again later.

The birthday-cake icing, thick and shockingly pink, was left lying there, on his aunt's plate.

That one, she'd always put on airs, nothing ever good enough for her. And like that since she was little. She hadn't put on more weight, had she? When one thought of the little girl she once was . . .

The nostalgic glorification of his aunt's beauty as a child meant the evening was drawing to a close, those anecdotes Anton knew off by heart: when she was barely twelve, and men would turn around as she passed. On Sunday evenings, when the fridge was empty, she'd go and ring the neighbor's doorbell and wheedle a snack out of him, and she wasn't yet nine. One day, her mother hadn't paid the dance center, so she went and sniveled in the director's office, convincing him to give her one month's free classes. She was a cheeky one, that Betty. A seductress. Who made adults drop like flies. She knew what she wanted, for sure . . .

At eleven, to pay for her private dancing lessons, she got up at 5:30 A.M. on Sundays, the market stallholder paid her in cash. She babysat for the neighbors. Never complained about a thing.

If she hadn't blown it, it would be a different story today . . .

At the door, his grandmother had given Anton a big hug, she was proud of him, it made up for all the rest.

Anton, his mouth still tasting of meat fat and mint toothpaste, had had a restless night. The alarm clock had gone off, dawn was breaking, seizing a patch of sky behind the grayish buildings.

At the breakfast table, Anton told his father that he was pleased he'd aroused his aunt's interest. Maybe he'd pay her a visit one of these days.

Sometimes he envied her, his father replied, she lived like a child. No alarm clock, no taxes, jobs now and then. She'd always done as she fancied, never worrying about the consequences: like that Wednesday when she'd left him, her eight-year-old little brother, waiting at the school gates. He'd gone to wait in the janitor's office. She'd shown up two hours later, on her fiancé's arm: so sorry, she hadn't noticed the time go by . . .

Could they just stop using the word "fiancé"?

Despite the interrogative form of her sentence, Anton's sister Dafina wasn't asking a question. The family version of the *story* made her sick, but now that Anton had a PhD in feminism, no doubt he'd be allowed to question it, this *story*. She stood up abruptly, put her cup in the sink, and disappeared into her bedroom.

I've upset your sister, his father sighed.

It had to be put into context: in the eighties, a very young girl could fall in love with a middle-aged man without there being an outcry. Marc had given her a lot of support. He'd virtually educated her, bought her clothes, books . . . Not all young girls were lucky enough to happen upon an educated, caring fiancé. Without Marc's help, and that grant he'd helped her to get, she wouldn't have had the means to prepare for that European competition in Antwerp. He'd even stood surety for their mother when she'd moved into a more spacious apartment. And anyhow, when Betty was a teenager, she was no saint or softie! The day of her audition for the Bordeaux theater, as soon as she saw the long line of dancers, she'd used the excuse of urgently needing the bathroom and, once inside the theater, had slipped on leotard, tights, and pointe shoes, and had been one of the first to dance for the choreographer, who had hired her. As for that way she'd had of just throwing it all away . . . a princess's caprice.

Anton had half-opened his big sister's bedroom door and found her sitting cross-legged on her bed, laptop on knees.

Any good at mental arithmetic, Anton? When Dad was eight, Betty was thirteen. That guy, around forty. *Fiancé*? No wonder Betty's screwy.

But . . . maybe Betty was in love with Marc? Anton had ventured.

Clearly, the family tradition was being perpetuated . . . Talking *about* Betty, but not *with* Betty. Exactly what she and Anton were doing right now. Go and see her, Dafina had whispered.

A nton imagined himself ringing Aunt Betty's doorbell and answering her questions about "*Mitou*," but first he'd have to sit facing a frowning Robin-shaped barrier. Robin, who never took his eye off Anton's aunt when they were at a family gathering, like a gardener concerned at seeing his favorite plant exposed to gusts of wind.

The previous week, the French teacher had asked them to comment on an extract from a book by Imre Kertész, *The Pathseeker*. The pupils grumbled: it made no sense, the narrator was returning to a town to look for evidence, but of what?

Anton had underlined a sentence saying that *he had always looked for what was being hidden from him, instead of seizing the visible.*

It didn't take him long to track Betty down on the net: she was the only Animalêtre volunteer to live in Fontenay and have a "friend" called Robin.

As her avatar, "Coppélia" had chosen the photo of a black ballerina in a red-and-gold tutu, who, Anton discovered, was called Misty Copeland, the first African-American soloist at the American Ballet Theatre.

Betty-Coppélia had four thousand friends. And each one seemed deserving of her compassion. She scattered emojis around messages from owners distraught at having lost their dog or cat: praying hands, thumbs up when a pet was found. They thanked her profusely, amazed at her kindness, her efficiency: thanks Coppélia, thanks to you I found my baby you watch over our darlings only you can understand my distress.

Coppélia dispensed advice and consolation, found solutions, searched, encouraged.

Coppélia had "liked" the pages of other volunteers, of veterinarians, of a star physiotherapist. Looking at her page, it was impossible to give an age to Coppélia. His aunt, with her collar like starched wings, whom everyone at the table had pretended to listen to for a few moments, the way one puts up with a little girl's prattle while waiting to put her to bed. His aunt whom everyone spoke of in the conditional, Betty who should have, Betty who could have, if only Betty hadn't.

R obin's reply to Anton's email, although hardly enthusiastic, hadn't taken long: if he didn't mind trekking over to Fontenay, they could have tea together at around 4 P.M.

The RER tracks were invisible from the window of Betty's and Robin's apartment, but on very windy days, the robotic voice announcing delays and passenger accidents even reached the sitting room; adopting the suave voice of the train company's announcer, Robin had asked to be excused, he had some calls to make.

With his left foot numb under his weight as he sat cross-legged on the sofa for almost an hour, Anton didn't move, dreading the ring of his mobile phone, the sounds of arguing in the street, the dripping of a tap, anything that might have disturbed Betty. His aunt was talking, not about what Anton wanted, but she was talking.

She may not have slept all night, but at least she'd succeeded in finding a family for a twelve-year-old stray dog; no one wanted to adopt elderly dogs. People anticipated the animal dying soon, they dreaded the sadness to come. She and Robin had adopted an old German pointer, years ago. It understood the slightest tweak of the lead, so it could avoid any obstacles on its walk. Adults urged Betty to euthanize it, it pained them to see it "in that state." But children were in raptures over its "beautiful clear blue eyes," the opaque eyes of the blind.

Betty was the human equivalent of an old, lame dog: a fat woman of around fifty who didn't dye her hair. Anton stammered that she wasn't old, wasn't fat, and . . . Betty interrupted him with a laugh: of course she was. And it didn't bother her. In fact, she rather liked it, getting old. In the street, men walked past without seeing her. Becoming invisible wasn't a death, but, quite the opposite, a rebirth, a new childhood. The proof: even her body was reverting to youth, she no longer got her periods.

Embarrassed, Anton lowered his eyes. Betty's bare feet on the kitchen floor tiles were proof of a past existence, the highly arched feet of a dancer. Her loose hair was punctuated with brown and gray spirals and commas, right down her back. She smiled at him. What would he like to know about dancing? Was it for school? Anton had almost forgotten about this pretext to justify his visit.

As though searching for animal tracks, the women of the family were always on the lookout for hair growth between dyeing sessions, shuddering: "My roots are showing." They kept out of the sun in summer, covered their faces in total sunblock, protecting their melanin level as though from a virus.

By her mere presence, his aunt with the long curls undermined the blond reinvention Anton's mother and grandmother put themselves through.

By her mere presence, his aunt undermined the reinvention of a *story* that Anton had meant to tackle. But allegiance to a family meant accepting a bunch of rules that you found you knew without ever having learnt them. That you found yourself applying.

That sentence Anton had repeated to himself in the train, in the elevator up to Betty's and Robin's apartment, he didn't say it: I have the answer to your *"Mitou"* questions.

Once outdoors, he had turned around: Betty was there, at the window, waving at him, a plucky little girl.

In his room, after supper, Anton took a look at Coppélia's web page. She'd posted a new photo, a grizzly dog found in a hypermarket car park, a vehicle must have struck it, its left back leg was turned inwards. As a caption, Betty had added just one word, in capitals: RESCUE. His aunt left jobs, discussions, a past, dinners. The only thing permanent about Betty was virtual, Coppélia's loyalty to those without a voice. Anton's burning heart was pounding, right up to his temples, when he clicked on the image of the black ballerina in a red tutu: would Coppélia accept his friend request? Would they see each other again next Wednesday?

How did you manage to find me, despite my pseudonym? His aunt, on opening the door to him, seemed amused, her slightly crooked front teeth making her look like a pretty, light-eyed marmot.

Anton had brought some cakes and a single question; the answer didn't really interest him, but at least he managed to ask it: the grant that had helped Betty's career take off, did it still exist? Had it been given to any famous dancers?

Robin had leant towards him, seeming disconcerted: excuse me?

The grant had helped nothing, she hadn't obtained it, his aunt had said. And then she'd gone quiet. A peal of church bells, police sirens, the rumble of a train, and children squealing upstairs all blended into an urban symphony. Robin had checked his watch, so Anton had mentioned some urgent homework to finish, mortified at having taken the wrong path. Once outdoors, he had turned around: she was there, at the window, waving at him, the sleeves of her cream-collared orange blouse flapping around her wrists, a butterfly.

H e had let two weeks go by, and then suggested visiting again, no longer bothering with pretexts.

On Wednesday afternoons, the three of them took the family path in reverse, over pastries washed down with liters of tea.

His aunt told him tales of abandonment: she orchestrated meetings between those she called non-human people and human beings. Betty's task was to put an end to straying, denounce ill-treatment, question those wishing to adopt, flush out any inconsistencies, organize car-sharing. How sad it all is, Anton sighed. Stories that had a beginning and an end weren't sad, his aunt replied. Unlike those that stagnated, in which nothing was clear, named.

As for his aunt, she wasn't sad at all. And could be quite caustic: to Anton, who'd complained about the cowardice of one pupil at school with Moroccan roots not defending another, a Romanian, who was being racially attacked, Betty had objected that, blond as he was, Anton wasn't risking much by being indignant, unlike the pupils concerned.

Betty was delighted that she was soon going hiking in the Puy-de-Dôme with Robin. Walking aimlessly fueled by excessively sweet brioches—that was the pleasure and privilege of competition losers, and she was proud to be one, with no life plan and on welfare.

When she won a game of Yahtzee, his aunt leapt up, then sat back down again, feigning modesty with an ethereal pose, like in that old photo of her as a child.

*

On his return, Anton's father questioned him: so, how was Betty?

The face his sister made when he admitted he hadn't yet found "the right moment" to bring up the questions asked on the evening of his birthday.

I t was Betty who chose that right moment. The following Wednesday, straight off, at the door: she had three things to say to him.

The first, she'd already told him but was keen to repeat it: she owed nothing to the Galatea grant.

The second was on her computer.

For the third, she took Anton's hand and held it between hers: if he preferred not to know, not to be put in an awkward position with the rest of the family, she'd understand. And wouldn't show him the web page.

APPEAL FOR WITNESSES

Between 1984 and 1994, you were around twelve years old. You were approached by a woman inviting you to apply for a grant from a "Galatea Foundation."

After an initial selection process, it was suggested that you attend a lunch to meet the members of the judging panel.

We would like to hear your story. Those interested in doing so can participate in a documentary on the Galatea affair. The first meeting will take place on Sunday, January 27 (details below).

By clicking on the link below, you will be redirected to a site that doesn't record IP addresses. So your answers to the questions will remain anonymous. If you don't wish to answer a particular question, move on to the next one.

Furthermore, whatever the distance in time, whatever the circumstances, and whoever may be implicated, the police encourage all those who have any information concerning the Galatea Foundation to testify by writing to the following email address:
temoignagegalatea-ocrteh@interieur.gouv.fr

IN WHAT WAY DO YOU THINK YOUR TESTIMONY COULD HELP US?

SURNAME: *if you don't wish to answer this question, go to the next one.*

FIRST NAME: *if you don't wish to answer this question, go to the next one.*

Betty told him of her sense of danger at that first farce of a selection process in front of the pseudo-judges, she was twelve and a half, of her certainty that she'd manage to get what she needed and avoid "the rest." How flattered she'd felt, too, that one of them, Marc, showed so much interest in her.

The mantra of shrinks, everything must be put into words, Betty didn't give a toss about that: she'd never tell Anton what "the rest" entailed. That, too, was her freedom.

After countless labyrinths, Betty had come to realize that there were just two paths: forgetting or forgiving.

But who to forgive, when she'd seen so many culprits, so many accomplices? Some of them coldly zealous, like Cathy.

The girl who'd introduced her to Cathy wasn't even that, an accomplice. She was a creature crazed with anxiety, a creature looking for a way out.

Anton hadn't asked a single question, apart from: would Betty respond to the appeal for witnesses?

His magical, lunatic aunt liked to cover up, leave out, and run away. Robin glanced at his watch, it was time for Anton to go home.

By chance, and thanks to a "*Mitou*" question that Anton had never answered, he had an opportunity to unravel the *story*, to get rid of the italics. He had the right, or duty, to do so.

Families were like those customers at hypermarkets who filled their carts with Chinese toys and jeans made in Pakistan, perfectly aware of the conditions in which these items had been manufactured. Family was where knowing and forgetting combined: the forgetting that was crucial to keep filling up those carts.

Each family gave rise to a unique language. Certain words drifted around, persistently, like fog. *A complicated story.* Others had a somber weightiness. *Move on to something else.* Families all knew the formula for tainted words: when found to be too harsh, they were plunged into a concentrate of denial until only an outline remained, that of a *fiancé*.

Betty had talked to him, but nothing had changed. Anton sat at his adolescent's place at the table, chewing what he was served until all he could hear was the grinding of molars reducing matter to mush.

He was chewing over what now seemed obvious: the erasing of the *story* was down to combined effort, familial solidarity. And the constant concern for the Betty-with-no-future made the question raised by a past Betty disappear. The Betty they'd all encouraged to prance ahead like a little clockwork horse. To become the representative of a prestigious France of white swans, a model of integration through classical ballet; all that was certainly worth a few silences. Betty, the thoroughbred in a family of the bedazzled. A blind family. Betty who had clenched her teeth and fists until she came of age.

Betty who was begrudged like some misleading ad for a great investment that turned out to be mediocre.

After supper, Anton asked his father and sister to join him in his room. He read them the appeal for witnesses. If Betty didn't reply, then he would.

Appropriating a past that didn't belong to him? And all because, on the evening of his birthday, she'd shown interest in a topical issue?

In what way did he think that, at his age, he was capable of sizing up what state his aunt was in, had he considered the consequences on the person he was claiming to "help?" What if Betty's silence had become her place of choice, the shady nook of a sanctuary?

He must resist the desire to draw the spotlight onto himself by "helping." And damned awful idea, shining that light recklessly on a woman who kept herself cloistered in her virtual world. Couldn't his sister just finally be left in peace, Anton's father had muttered, as he snapped the bedroom door shut.

Sitting beside Anton, Dafina took his hand.

■ ■ ■

IN WHAT WAY DO YOU THINK YOUR TESTIMONY COULD HELP US?

The cursor hovering on the page, like the needle of scales unable to gauge the weight of Anton's decision.

if you don't wish to answer this question, go to the next one.

8

T he Galatea Foundation affair (see our issues of September 19 and 20) is back in the spotlight due to the file found on the computer of an alleged member of the network, a former "judge" within the foundation. This file contains more than four hundred photos of young girls selected, since 1984, for that fictional grant.

Due to the scale of the affair, it has been decided that an appeal for witnesses should be made among those women who were approached by that foundation.

A toll-free phone number and an email address— temoignagegalatea-ocrteh@interieur.gouv.fr—have been made available. Analysis of the photos logged in the Europol database is underway. Obtaining the testimony of the now-adult victims will be crucial to the continuation of the inquiry. Two complaints lodged by parents in 1990 and 1992 were not pursued due to a lack of proof. The testimony of one victim, designated as "0.2" in the file, stated that there was a system of recruitment among the victims themselves, across several schools in the eastern suburbs of Paris. The fear of being questioned as procurers has probably contributed to the silence of the victims, most of whom come from working-class or dysfunctional families.

Alongside the inquiry, another appeal for witnesses has been launched on the Facebook page of the production company ELVENID, as it prepares to film a documentary on the subject.

Libération *newspaper*

S itting cross-legged on the sheets, Cléo examines her night the way one prods a limb after a fall. Not a trace, in her dreams, of the article read the previous day, no figure appearing from the past, not even a setting—the Collège Jean-Macé, the RER train, the Place de la Mairie, where the skating rink looked more like a swamp from spring onwards, the stagnant whiff coming from slimy weeds stuck to the gray stone.

A slow, empty night, untainted by the year 1984. On the table in the sitting room, the computer taunts her, its screen's flat face ready to log the slightest request, with zeal.

Dysfunctional families. Broken. Working-class.

She has no sociological excuse. No excuse of any sort.

She opens wide the French door overlooking the street, to break the stuffy silence of the apartment. In the square opposite, parents rig out their children as if for an imminent catastrophe: helmet, elbow pads, knee guards. They equip their teenagers with phones that track them, steal the passwords of their internet accounts, priding themselves on their vigilance. Cléo thinks of the dead angle, where no parent will hear Cathy's sweet music coming. Cléo thinks of the signs missed, of the scent of predictable disasters.

Somewhere there exists a photograph of a thirteen-year-old Cléo, a Galatea candidate, archived for all eternity.

The precise order in which events occurred has been

blurred by the passing years. The past is a landscape hazy as a speckled print, mapped out on the pages of a blue notebook, stored under the marital bed along with back issues of *Elle* magazine.

Barely a dozen pages, filled with first names and dates, underlined with a ruler: Marjorie O.K. Wednesday April 12, 2 P.M. Cendrine O.K. Wednesday April 19/26, 2 P.M.

Her Chosen Ones. *You can sniff out talent.*

The acrid dryness in her mouth since the previous day; that twisting of her innards, the weight of an aching mass right down her back. Let it be done with, let them judge her and punish her.

For years, she crossed the street, turned tail, thinking she recognized *a judge, someone very important for your future*.

For years, that tightening of the throat over a smell, a word: *frigid. Opium. Gift*.

For years, at the merest glance lingering on her, in the metro, the bus, at a birthday party, in the aisles of a store, at parents' meetings, feeling sure she'd been recognized. *Weren't you at the Collège Jean-Macé?*

This exhausting monologue, known only to her, a creaking carousel with a clatter of words without anyone to stop it, anyone to go right back to the beginning of the tale and calmly examine the facts, to absolve her, or perhaps condemn her, so that at least the *story* would be brought to a close.

That *story* is a splinter over which her skin regrew as the years passed. A little pink cushion of life, solid and springy. That foreign body is no longer foreign, it belongs to her, firmly held in a bundle of muscle fibers, barely eroded by time.

Her husband and their daughter offered her the chance of a path that she gratefully took, a satin ribbon, a skillful combination of threads, weft and warp, woven into a silky sheen. Cléo worked relentlessly on smoothing that path, removing, as she went along, any minuscule fragments of splinter. Relentlessly.

S unlight fills the room, starkly wan, blanking out the computer screen. Through the window, in the building's garden, the poplar gently sways, rustling like crumpled tissue paper. It's November, but autumn is hesitating to start, the humid warmth of morning lingering until evening. The flowers on the balcony are wilting, shriveling up; her husband and daughter take her to task like a child: she must have watered them too much, or not enough—with her, everything spoils, from plants to spices past their use-by date at the back of the kitchen cupboard.

They're united in their plant know-how, wearing pink rubber gloves, pruning, pulling things up; she sweeps the balcony's tiled floor after them, I'm your minion, she says, amused, your laborer. They both know so many things that she can never remember: the month for planting dahlias, how to make a béchamel sauce without butter, which kitchen drawer the scissors are kept in, when to book train tickets for the best price, the title of the first book of *À la Recherche du Temps Perdu*. This alliance of Lucie with her father touches her. The roles are shared out: for her husband, domestic glory for his scallop soufflés and the flower-filled balcony; for her, a glory archived on the Institut National de l'Audiovisuel website, taped on VHS cassettes stored in a shoebox.

A "glory" she has carefully expurgated of one particular episode, the way dictatorships erase the figure of a traitor from official photos.

*

Her daughter had said the word "mommy" for the first time while pointing at the TV screen. The little girl begged to watch them again, those recorded compilations of Cléo's TV appearances between 1990 and 1999.

The Evian ad: second dancer from the right, in a short, white A-line dress, *Mommy!* The dancer with an auburn bob, *that's Mommy*, swirling between Parisian-café tables for Guess. On the set of the TV program *Stars 90*, in black shorts, third dancer from the left behind Mylène Farmer, *Mommy, Mommy!* Her daughter stamped her feet as soon as the song's intro began, knew the refrain by heart, *tout est chaos, à côté, tous mes idéaux, des mots abîmés.* Her daughter always recognized her. In a blond wig. Made-up as a geisha, kimono, hair straightened and bangs in eyes. Behind a superheroine mask, bouncy brown curls topped with Wonder Woman headdress. Among a group of some twenty dancers. Lucie would point her finger at the screen, *you're there.*

Cléo imagines her husband and daughter in front of her: *There's something I have to tell you.*

Would they wear the same disapproving expression as when they find moldy food she's forgotten at the back of the fridge?

Would they be, in this order: staggered, incredulous, disgusted? Or would they feel sorry for her, that thirteen-year-old Cléo?

But what sympathy could you feel for a girl who said nothing, ever, out of exemplary loyalty to Cathy? That loyalty of more than thirty years.

There's something I have to tell you.

Too easy to take the role of the victim.

Laurence O.K. Wednesday April 12, 2 P.M. Nathalie O.K. Wednesday April 19/26, 2 P.M.

About the lunches, *the* lunch, she'd say nothing.
the fingers the insects relax
Their disgust. Her shame.

She would explain, without looking for excuses, without blaming the slightest *dysfunctional family*, that she'd protected herself as best she could, that she'd done what she'd been asked to do. Asked? Or suggested: *Only if it's O.K. with you, Cléo.*

A dependable entrepreneur of thirteen years, six months, and three days old, surrounded by pleading girls.

The "0.2" of the article in *Libération* might be one of them, who won't have forgotten Cléo—how could she possibly forget Cléo?—who'd be interviewed and would point out the guilty one with a steady hand: *You're here, Cléo.*

The Paula of the lunch, Cathy's "indispensable assistant," is she "0.1"? Or is there a Paula from before Paula? Who wrote names down in a notebook like Cléo did. An endlessly recurring figure.

0.1 strain of a devastating virus. 0.1 sad queen of an anonymous herd. 0.1 first of the Chosen Ones. Favorite. Cog in the machine, victim and culprit, a martyr-torturer. This same monologue for years on end.

You're there. Right, Mommy?

...

In grade school, to the question "mother's profession," her daughter loved answering: "dancer." This white lie (Cléo had quit dancing when Lucie was four) had allowed her to muster a court around her: from third to sixth grade, regularly, a few pupils were allowed to visit the apartment-turned-museum. With the blasé confidence of a guide, Lucie would open wide her mother's cupboard: there, the Lycra gear, here, a *sudisette*, those plastic-coated sweat suits for warming the muscles. She held out dresses protected in gray covers; this one, drenched in pearls, had been given to Cléo by the producers after shooting a video for the band Niagara. Her daughter avoided naming performers as soon as they no longer seemed famous enough to her: out went Paula Abdul, out went Ace of Base. Her daughter edited her career so it featured no failed prestigious auditions (Angelin Preljocaj hadn't hired her, she lacked classical technique; Prince's manager had found her too "nondescript" to dance behind the singer in concert). Lucie stressed the hours of rehearsal required for the three-minute performance that Michel Drucker would wrap up by saying: *The dancers will now leave the set.*

One girl had been amazed to find, in Cléo's portfolio, the Diamantelles program of 1999. The little girls' incredulous expressions: like on the TV, on New Year's Eve?

Cléo would give them all a fruit juice, it was snack time;

she'd answer any questions: dancing in a cabaret meant being able to go from a waltz to a modern-jazz routine. And you weren't really naked. Although, in her eyes, there was nothing shameful about nudity.

Barely had her friends left before Lucie had rushed into her room in tears, like some exhibition curator who'd just discovered that her favorite painting is a fake.

C léo had been invited in by Lucie's teacher: one didn't often get the chance to hear a dancer-mom's story. *At what age did you start?*

At what age, the discovery that, by being watched, one could extricate oneself from the passing of time, speed things up, and finally break free? At what age had that need to be *spotted* become pressing?

At what age did you start?

Mostly, she'd had to start over.

At fourteen, *after*, a new Cléo, going to a new school, had joined a new dance class in Paris, far from the youth and culture center. She had, *in the end*, been lucky. From now on, she would be exemplary. From now on, she would hone her dance skills like an artisan, and would serve dance, entirely detached from honors, titles, or rewards.

Much to her parents' displeasure, she'd turned down the offer of participating in a TV report on FR3 that would follow the progress of three trainee dancers. Had given up the prospect of dancing solo in the end-of-year show, on the pretext of a painful tendon. None of all that bothered her, quite the opposite. Each of these sacrifices purified her, emptiness soothed her, like water drunk upon waking, that ice-cold liquid slipping down the esophagus.

Her interior monologue had died down, now only flickering weakly, like a worn-out light bulb. In the time it took her to believe in *starting over*, Cléo had a taste of the banality of a schoolgirl adolescence. An interval of delightful squabbles with Yonasz—how on earth could Cléo claim that Jean-Jacques Goldman was a poet?—an interval lit by candles, on the evening of the Sabbath, at the table of Serge and Danuta, where words had the sweep of a landscape, the subtleties of a poem: *in the absence of forgiveness, let oblivion come.*

Cléo's mother stated that you could tell "the right sort of people" by their perfectly straight teeth and the sales receipts they didn't keep. She was wrong: it was by their rapid loss of interest in what was no longer of use to them. That large drawer into which Yonasz chucked songs, T-shirts he'd tired of, and her—all no longer of any interest.

He had loved her, agreeing to everything. And had dropped her the moment she'd expressed disagreement with him. She was barely sixteen. The school, with its corridors and rectangular yard, had turned into a trap with a suffocating smell: a pupil in her class had discovered a little *something* about her. It might have been a coincidence. Or else: the girl *knew*.

A tart who sucks off old men

How could she have imagined that it would be any different? That it would be so easy? As if a weekly phone call to her grandparents, visiting a sick classmate, and handing her essays in on time could have been enough. (*Sniggering from the interior monologue.*)

She still had to pay. The Galatea account wasn't closed.

Daily life without Yonasz had been a gaping hole Cléo had fallen into. Her interior monologue triumphed, reverberating once more in her every vertebra, with Cléo unable to stifle the echoes: nothing, no offering, would ever be enough.

The past was irreversible. No forgiveness could undo what had been.

S he was nineteen. One audition followed another: Cléo was too tall, too short, her thighs too muscular, bust not big enough, bust too big, didn't have enough classical technique. These setbacks calmed her, she still had to pay.

Her parents worried, fearing she'd never manage to earn a living. Cléo herself knew that she'd

known how to go about getting remunerated

On Saturday evening, her mother laid the coffee table in the sitting room, with bowls of peanuts and Tuc crackers, unnaturally pink taramasalata, and a portion of brie. The theme music of *Champs-Élysées* was starting: with all three of them squeezed on the sofa, sitting on breadcrumbs, her mother pointed out a dancer on the screen: that one, she was in the Malko company, but danced less well than Cléo. She mustn't lose hope. As her heart contracted with love and sorrow, Cléo rolled her eyes, what nonsense, squashed between her mother who *didn't know* and her father who *didn't know*.

He commented on the singers' performances, nudging Cléo with his elbow, hey, there's your beloved Goldman, *Aurais-je été meilleur ou pire que ces gens*, only to be scolded with a vigorous SHUSH from his wife. The phone rang but went unanswered, her mother absent-mindedly plaited Cléo's hair, a child-Cléo, longing to be tucked in, protected, and lacking any kind of plan B.

P lan A had, finally, materialized, a cryptic notice pinned up in a dance center: "For TV promos and filming of video clip, seek dancers, modern-jazz technique, between 1m 60cm and 1m 70cm."

Three whispering people sitting in the darkness of the empty Mogador theater had pointed at her, plucked her out from the rows of girls: *You, number 51. A bit tall, but energetic. Leave your photo.*

She didn't have one. How did she think she'd work without a photo? Did she think she was unforgettable, or what?

Cléo had sat on the grass in a park close to the Gare de l'Est until the groundskeeper directed her to the exit; the ground, sandy gray and cracked, was littered with beer-bottle caps and dried dog turds.

That evening, she'd made an appointment with the recommended photographer, canceled it, and then called back. Before knocking on the studio door, she'd popped a quarter of a tranquillizer pill, filched from the drawer of her father's bedside table.

Next, ten photos had to be selected from the proof sheet, she'd left it up to the photographer. That confident, wily, arching girl, who *could sniff out talent*, left her aghast, disgusted her, so ugly. *Sick.*

Cléo had been hired for the promo of Mylène Farmer's new single: "Disillusioned Generation." She'd be positioned at the back, to the left, so as not to be taller than the singer.

She'd felt like telling Yonasz about it first, to hear him crack up laughing: the "pop songs" he despised had just recognized her, from now on, she was a "pro."

At the table, her parents talked about nothing else. About the costumes. About Mylène. About setting the alarm at 5 A.M. for a breakfast-TV program. About the cover of *Télé 7 Jours*, with the singer surrounded by her dancers.

The choreographer had shared a little "trick" with Cléo: for TV shows, she should imagine, behind the camera, an audience of her loved ones, the people she really wanted to dance for.

Yonasz and Serge were central to this imaginary audience, from which Cléo kept having to dispel the image of Cathy.

M alko's stocky figure, that compact chest under the tracksuit jacket that gaped when he demonstrated a *port de bras*, had had that power: of silencing, or almost, Cléo's interior monologue. Reducing it to a whisper.

He was smaller than he looked on TV, she'd told her mother over the phone. The atmosphere at the course, in Bordeaux, was ghastly: a continuous battle to attract the attention of a star choreographer and be hired in his company. There were more than fifty of them packed into the rehearsal room, its mirrored walls coated in a sticky mist of sweat, and they barely spoke in the changing rooms.

And in the evening, what do you do, go for a walk? her father asked.

In the evening, she lay rigid on her bed. A circuit devoid of electricity, but with flashes of throbbing pain. Stiffness, she knew all about. But not these involuntary spasms of the thigh muscles, or the knotting in the pit of the abdomen, like a cramp that won't let up, or the bruised knees, as if she'd hurled herself onto concrete.

Malko demanded that they throw themselves across the floor as if it were "an enemy to destroy, a lover to reconquer." Cléo wore two pairs of woolly tights under her sweatpants as a kind of protection.

Repeat repeat repeat.

They all felt nauseous as they emerged from classes. They all spoke of that moment when, finally, they no longer knew what their body was doing, and when they "repeated," despite what a pounding heart was telling them.

On the third day of the course, Malko had screamed STOP, paused the CD, and then pointed at Cléo: *You, at the back, with the long hair, come here. Think you're on the beach? Move it! Repeat.*

Without music, in front of everyone, Cléo had launched into it. *Step step* AND *tilt* AND: a total blank. Nothing. Cléo couldn't remember the steps anymore, so she'd improvised, then stopped, bangs plastered to forehead, throat parched.

Well, well now. Why bother to learn my choreo? Do your own thing, it's so much better!

Cléo had to admit that, sorry, she'd forgotten one or two transition steps.

He held her by the shoulders, displaying her to the others: this was what he wanted. A girl neither very beautiful, nor very strong technically. Who had the guts to keep going, no matter what, if she forgot. The fucking guts to improvise. To carry on as if.

He'd only asked her her name on the last day: *Good work, Cléo.*

Three words that were like an orchestral finale, the jubilation of triumphant chords, she was dancing on air: she did good work! Malko's approval lessened the persistent pain at the back of her thigh, a pulled muscle she'd treated with a painkiller in the morning, an ice pack at bedtime. It was worth it. She did good work. The interior monologue receding, quieting down.

H ired by the company on a trial basis. Every day, from 11 A.M. to 7 P.M., Malko was observing her, frowning, yeah: need to check under the hood. He delved inside Cléo, open-stomach surgery, the big clean-out. What she thought she knew: ditch it. And don't bother with that tragic look. What on earth did Cléo imagine? That people drained from working all day wanted to see, on stage, a little creature who apologized for existing? They were going to spend money on her! She must respect their money! No one gave a shit about her doubts, her fears! She could keep them for her retirement, it'd give her something to do.

Cléo's relief at leaving the monologue to him, her desire, her hope that he'd cure her of it.

Malko taught her instability, "almost falling." He played with space as if it were a game of chance. Barely had one movement been suggested than another one interrupted it; Malko superimposed pirouettes on grands jetés. Panting: I can't, not at that speed. Slowly, he dissected the mechanics of the movement: you can. One could.

Maybe it was the effect of those sudden stops in full flight, Malko's sense of syncopation. A dancer whose sister studied neuroscience claimed that their elation, and their insomnia, too, was all chemical, the result of cerebral hemispheres satisfying opposing demands. Their ecstasy at managing to do this boosted them. They were high on adrenaline.

Her mother had come to watch a rehearsal. On the way out,

with tears in her eyes: how could Cléo put up with that? What need was there to scream like that! Calling her daughter a fat cow!

Cléo threw herself into this maelstrom with passion. Malko was training them in resistance, even to him. Neither very beautiful, nor very strong technically, but gutsy.

Nothing could ever be taken for granted: you were the favorite for three days running, on the fourth, for just one mistake, you were relegated to the back of the room.

He was rewriting her.

Cléo was tall? He demanded that she acquire the speed of a short girl. Cléo was supple and willowy? He wanted her to be powerful, springy, making her lift dancers weighing eighty kilos. When she emerged from the shower, in front of the mirror, she recognized, here and there, traces of who she once was: an over-slender neck, skinny forearms. Her biceps bulged, her stomach, when she lifted her sweater, delighted her brother: just like Robocop's!

Malko announced it to her at the end of a rehearsal: the gentle engagement period was over, time to move on to the nuptials, until tendonitis do us part, Cléo was now part of the company. She was twenty-one, she'd be the youngest among those whom France on a Saturday night called "Malko's dancers."

They'd all arrive together at Studio Gabriel, at midday, all leave together shortly after midnight. Fifteen handcrafted dancers Malko watched over: he went to every dressing room, checking that they had enough bottles of water, black and herbal tea, fresh and dried fruit, dark chocolate, heating, but no more than twenty degrees, clean towels, massage oils.

He paced up and down on the set, went among the technicians and the cables, demanded warmer lighting, asking to check the framing, livid if he discovered a close-up of a dancer's buttocks or breasts.

We're not at the butcher's here, I don't want you chopping them up in pieces.

The head cameraman protested, it was his program, after all; Malko shouted, threatened, fetch the director, the producer. Immediately. Or he'd be off. With the girls.

He watched out for any intense looks from the singers, turned them away when they came looking for the dancers' dressing rooms. He worried about a glass floor, they'd slip; spent the night cutting out tiny pieces of thin felt to stick on the tip of high-heeled shoes. He worried about the hours spent going over sequencing under the heat of the spotlights, poured them drinks before they got thirsty.

When, at 8:30 P.M., Drucker announced: *And now, please welcome the dancers*, Cléo would spot Malko in the wings, hands gripped, mouthing every single step.

I t wasn't unusual, in the metro, for teenagers sitting opposite Cléo to whisper to their mother that she was "the redhead" off the Drucker show. The redhead with the high ponytail, whose name and photo featured in its program: *The Ballets de Malko Live*. Audiences cheered them, in Lille, in Toulouse, insatiable for those swift bodies. Audiences that knew her, recognized her: when she arrived on stage, Cléo was welcomed with joyous cries and whistles. In a tuxedo and high heels, she pressed her hips against her partner's, wrapped her thighs around another dancer's pelvis. Dancing sex was mathematical, every movement counted out, *arch 7 turn 8 AND*.

She was twenty-three, she was twenty-five, sex was mathematical, it was no big deal to her: a set engineer for three months, the stage manager of a Jeff Buckley concert for one night, a dancer's brother from time to time. She wasn't *frigid*. But her emotions lay elsewhere, an overwhelming emotion of tenderness and desire, aroused in her by the merest nape of a girl's neck. She'd have to wait, to love girls, for the shame to leave her, the shame of having betrayed them.

She was twenty-seven when she met Lara. She should have been able to arrive fresh to such a delightful love. She should have been able to ready herself to welcome it. She hadn't had the time, and Lara hadn't taken it.

Throughout their love affair, her mother had insisted on calling Lara "your roommate."

Cléo was twenty-eight in 1999, and the production companies were starting to prefer "movers" to dancers. Those who "moved well" were spotted in nightclubs and weren't concerned about fees, happy to be rewarded with fame: they'd appeared in *Big Brother* and were waiting impatiently for the auditions for *Loft Story*, methodically balancing out what they earned with what they invested in improvements to the "tool of their trade": breast implants, pec implants, dermabrasions, and nose jobs.

The TV shows the Malko dancers still featured in, were a celebration of nineties nostalgia. But their success endured on stage: every Saturday, the dancers would take the train for Petit Quevilly, Ambert, Soustons. A retired volunteer, hair sprayed as if for a wedding, would greet them enthusiastically at the station. They'd pile into the municipal minibus and, on the way, the volunteer would point out a church, a hiking path, they must come back for their holidays. A notice on A3 paper taped to the door of the auditorium heralded them: "This evening, EXCLUSIVELY! BALLETS MALKO (*Champs-Élysées, Lahaye d'honneur*, etc.)"

They were shown to the dressing rooms: two small rooms cluttered with plastic chairs pushed against the wall. They did their make-up, checked their hair in a pocket-mirror; the deputy mayor had laid out plates of *saucisson* and pâté for them, filling the room with a fatty smell of blood and salt.

The dancers put up with bumpy linoleum flooring, two

lateral spotlights, and speakers that distorted the bass. With showers that were too cold. And with Malko's absence.

After the show, young girls would linger around the dancers, hoping to be noticed. They held their skinny wrists out to Cléo: here, at the crook of the elbow, she should sign here. They left her little pieces of folded-up paper, an ardent secret, I always liked you best on TV, their phone numbers festooned with hearts, in case she ever came back one day. Their spontaneous trust, such sweetness to be exploited, left an aftertaste, in Cléo's mouth, of fear.

uditions were becoming rare. Choreographers glanced at her CV: sorry, they were looking for more "contemporary" girls. She would insist, I can do it all. You know how it is, Cléo, she'd hear them respond, you're a bit too obviously nineties sexy. Malko. Things have moved on.

It was only temporary, just to make some money: every Friday evening, from 11 P.M. to 4 A.M., Cléo would put on a white bikini and, perched on the Folies-Pigalle podium, would writhe on the spot, arms up, a sway to the right, then to the left, a twirl, nothing technical.

The revelers knew her by the name of Natacha. Behind the scenes, the girls advised Cléo to avoid telling any potential boyfriends that she was a go-go dancer. When men heard that, they imagined all sorts of things.

Barely out of the Folies, some girls would rush to Boulevard Rochechouart: peep shows every ten meters, thirty francs for a five-minute striptease: if you were well organized, it added up to a decent night's pay.

Cléo sometimes stood in for one, who was exhausted, or another, who had her period. She carried out her task seriously: these men, behind the glass, were an audience like any other and mustn't be disappointed.

To men who approached her at birthday parties, in cafés—would she like to see them again?—she didn't hide her precarious situation: she had little time to give them, and no money. They invited her to lunch, to dinner, paid for her taxi, for a dance-class voucher. No big deal, and no love.

Lara had stolen that word from her emotional landscape. Cléo was waiting to catch her interrupted breath. Cléo's mother wanted to know if she had "someone," soon it would be too late for a baby.

In autumn 1999, an audition for the prestigious show at the Diamantelles cabaret attracted two hundred dancers, all between 1m 76cm and 1m 80cm tall, who'd rushed over from Munich, Barcelona, or Nice.

Despite being only 1m 73cm, Cléo was hired as an under-study dancer. In her contract, it stipulated that, on stage, a smile and the false eyelashes supplied by the establishment were mandatory.

Within a fortnight, this setting became her cocoon: the white staircase garlanded with plastic wisteria, the crimson drapes, the marble, and the gilded stucco—more gold than one could handle, from the rims of the champagne glasses to the glittery powder Cléo dusted across the arch of her brows. The *meneuse de revue* had shown Cléo how to transform herself into a Diamantelle girl: that strict sequence of the products and colors to use.

Before going on stage, Cléo would ask another dancer to check, here, on her thigh: was she sure the birthmark couldn't be seen?

Cléo had been allocated a dresser. A lady clad in safe shades of brown called Claude, who'd suggested that Cléo remain with her back to her while she undressed and dressed her: it would be more "comfortable" like that.

On the phone, Cléo's mother had gotten annoyed at their closeness: she was forever mentioning that name, Claude seemed to have become her second mom!

Cléo had very nearly *told* her "second mom" everything. But the memory of Lara's expression once she *knew* had stopped her.

Lara would have been amazed to see Cléo joining a small group of stagehands and dancers concerned about the safety of a particular dancer. And to read the petition they'd drafted together. Lara would have understood Cléo's outraged hurt when Claude, her "second mom," had abandoned her: she hadn't signed the petition.

Almost two years after their split, Cléo still looked at whatever upset or pleased her through the Lara prism: would her "roommate" have been condescending towards, or sung the praises of, those Crazy Horse dancers who'd gone on a "smile strike" to get a salary increase?

Cléo told their story to Adrien on the evening they met, at a birthday party, in spring 2000: the smile as weapon. He thought it "adorable." But: had Cléo *really* danced in a revue?

He asked her questions without waiting for her answers, raved about both the Anatolian rug in their host's sitting room and the Savéol tomatoes in the salad. Authenticity! For Adrien, the twenty-first century would be that of the quest for the "real." He, for example, was prepared to travel many kilometers to savor grass-fed lamb or veal. He loved biographies for the same reason: novels, like shows, felt artificial to him.

Very soon, Adrien had wanted to introduce her to his "gang"; they'd all been at the Dijon business school together. Moments before entering the restaurant, he'd advised Cléo to avoid mentioning her Diamantelles experience, his buddies were prone to teasing.

He lived in a three-room apartment close to the Arts et Métiers metro station, where he left the heating on even when he was out, without worrying about the bill; he read her articles from both *Le Monde* and *Le Figaro*: being partisan was being blinkered, there was good everywhere, Right, Left, that was old hat. Cléo drove him into a corner: if he was on the jury in a trial, he'd be obliged to choose a side.

He frowned, got annoyed when she quibbled, shut her up with a kiss: he liked her better as a dancer than as an attorney.

Cléo had told Adrien about Lara, and he sometimes worried, after they'd made love, was it better with a girl? She didn't lie to him: it wasn't "better" with Lara. How was it, which adjectives to use, did they even exist?

One day, when strolling in the Marais district, they'd desired each other so much that they'd pushed open the door to a building and lain down behind the stairs on the bare, blue-tiled floor of the entrance hall. Her bare thigh against Lara's labia in sync with her tongue in Lara's mouth. That's how it was with Lara.

Cléo appreciated loving Adrien gently, with no urgency, no suffering, no fear of losing him. She liked the tranquility of not totally desiring him. She liked that he wanted to "protect" her, even if she no longer needed that.

Cléo imagined a drawer slotted between her floating ribs and her heart, containing figures and settings Adrien didn't know existed: Lara's kitchen, where Cléo had listened to the collective's debates; the corridor, at Yonasz's, that led to his father's study. The texts Serge had given her, stuck in her notebook, forgiveness. Opium. The Chosen Ones.

Every other Sunday, they had lunch with Cléo's parents. Her mother's eagerness was painful to behold. With a slash of coral blush on her cheeks and pumps on her feet, she minced over to the kitchen. She pronounced Vincennes as "Vinceeennes," the lengthened syllable containing both castle and forest, as if they didn't live in a block on the edge of Fontenay, with just one bus to the RER station, and only every twenty minutes at that. As if she wasn't one of those thousands of women over fifty-five who filled in temping-agency forms, and as if she didn't love to sing "Les Lacs du Connemara" in the car, as if her parents had ever been to the Musée d'Orsay, which Adrien much preferred to the Louvre. As if, on the maternal bedside table, there weren't piles of book-club novels and old issues of *Télé 7 Jours*.

Adrien frowned when Cléo exclaimed that cherries cost a fortune, and mocked her "skinflint" tendencies: buying train tickets way in advance, favoring a carafe of tap water over sparkling in restaurants. Her parents said nothing, embarrassed at hearing these family precepts criticized, and then her father would nod, one didn't discuss money at the table.

By winter 2001, she was pregnant. Adrien's friends had congratulated Cléo; she imagined them squashed between the two of them in the conjugal bed, applauding their prowess: his sperm bumping into her ovum.

Cléo wished she could ditch her skin. Free herself from this defeated body, one with no verve, far removed from that sweat-and-camphor routine: dance. Cléo felt permanently nauseous, was losing weight. Adrien insisted, she must make an effort, he kept a close eye on her fork, made her gratins, lasagnas, both easy to eat. His love was like a blanket, a protective tarp kept firmly fixed over a greenhouse with end-of-days temperatures.

All around her, the word "baby," repeated ad nauseam: moisturizing creams promising women the return of *baby-soft skin*. Critics moved by the *baby voice* of simpering female singers with palatal diction. On the cover of magazines, models styled like kids, with freckles drawn onto their *baby blushed* cheeks. Agencies offering parents an estimate of their earning potential, there's no right age to launch a child's modeling career. *Your little one will, however, need to be photogenic, amiable, with a harmonious, smiley face, and above all, be very well-behaved and obedient.*

Cléo would hear Adrien talking about her on the phone: he wasn't "necessarily that insistent" that she stop dancing, but he'd read that dancers' overdeveloped abs didn't help with giving birth, they found it hard *to relax.*

you must relax

She was expecting a girl. Sobbing for hours on end, locked in the bathroom, with no idea what she was crying about. Could you hope to educate one human being when you'd contributed to the destruction of another one, of several, maybe?

Present yourself as an example?

Do as Mommy does

Lucie was born, and Cléo couldn't manage to change her, feed her, rock this little wordless being, dependent on her. Sometimes, she dreamt she was cradling a little girl with Betty's face. Cléo could almost taste that flowery pink icing on the cake served by Betty's mother the first time she'd visited. Madame Bogdani's incongruous deference when welcoming Cléo.

The coiled telephone cable under Cléo's bedroom door. *Come on, Cléo!*

The dark eyebrows and clear eyes, the slightly crooked front teeth: Betty boasted about her "lucky teeth," merely shrugging when explained that she'd gotten it wrong.

Having done nothing said nothing but having let it all happen. Not even a hand placed on little Betty's shoulder.

N eeding help wasn't a sign of weakness, Adrien insisted, even if Cléo's parents had taught her that one could only count on oneself . . .

Could she blame her parents' life? A life spent "getting by" on their own. Could she blame them for passing on their passivity, those shrugs at any mention of petitions, strikes, mutual aid?

Could she blame the current chorus of slogans? The Galatea spirit was everywhere, may the best girl win, even in the way a colleague had announced his redundancy to Adrien: it would give him a *boost*!

Could one blame films, TV series, reality shows, the songs of her adolescence, *'cause everybody's living in a material world, and I am a material girl*?

Or maybe none of all that. She'd have to stay alone in that realm of shame, carrying the virus that lived inside her, which she had spread.

Valérie O.K. Wednesday April 12, 2 P.M. Sophie O.K. Wednesday April 19, 2 P.M.

P ushed by Adrien, Cléo had agreed to see a psychother-
apist, whose bookshelf overflowed with books in no
particular order, including that one on forgiveness:
L'Imprescriptible, by Vladimir Jankélévitch. A paperback copy,
like Serge's.

Serge and Yonasz. The sudden distress Cléo had felt in the
park when Yonasz had admitted he didn't want to be Jewish.
You couldn't just let go of their hands, you couldn't just drop
your ghosts.

The therapist had asked Cléo if there was any particular
subject she'd like to begin with.

Would she be absolved if she poured out that interior monologue to him? Forgiven? Would it be enough to exchange what
she'd done with a banknote placed in the shrink's hand?

Cléo had canceled the following appointment. She'd call
again.

In 2003, after several attempts to keep afloat, despite various injuries—to the meniscus, the quads, and then lumbago—Cléo had made an appointment at the job center.

At each of her interviews, her adviser seemed to forget that he'd already quoted La Fontaine's "The Cicada and the Ant" at her: *found herself sorely deprived when the North wind arrived.*

Why not do her diploma in teaching dance?

She didn't have a didactic bone in her body.

And yet, he objected, Cléo had had quite a career, it would be great to pass her experience on to young girls.

doing what Cléo does

Or then . . . masseuse, perhaps? Or—although it wasn't really relevant to her skill set—receptionist at a dance center in the Bastille area?

From 9 A.M. to 5 P.M., Cléo directed arrivals to the changing rooms, answered the phone, took payments. At the start of each lesson—the center had five halls—the pupils handed her their ticket, they all knew her by her first name, they confided in her: Cléo, you're way cooler than my mom, thanks, Cléo.

The manager praised her for her vigilance. One of Lucie's classmates had told her, in fits of laughter, about when her father, waiting for her after her street-jazz class, had been questioned at length by Cléo: how embarrassing that he'd been taken for a pedo. She was a fierce one, her mother.

Her daughter knew so many things that Cléo had never thought of. She seemed to have a giant compass to help her draw the boundaries between good, useless, positive, toxic; everything was molecules broken down to their basic structure. Lucie organized her life as though orchestrating a symphony, looking out for the slightest dissonance. She tested everything with the most cautious dip of a toe, never venturing into a restaurant before checking it was positively reviewed, and on several websites at that.

She'd just celebrated her nineteenth birthday but still enjoyed, on lazy Sunday afternoons, finding traces of Cléo on YouTube: her mother had fans, the "Malko special" videos clocked up thousands of recent views! Just like when she was a child, except that now, there was an edge to Lucie's laughter when she pointed at her mother on the screen. That outfit she was wearing, how kitsch is that! Those dancers—whether wearing a tutu to wait for a prince, or wiggling in satin mini-shorts—were bodies for hire, who never had a say, and never got offended about it.

Cléo nodded, maybe, darling. Maybe her daughter was right.

Cléo thought of Claude's workshop, of the rhinestones stitched onto the fabrics, the more facets a rhinestone had, the more directions it sparkled in, a blaze of open questions. Cléo had no answers.

Her daughter would never be for hire. She'd have cracked up laughing if, at thirteen, a grant for excellence had been dangled in front of her. She'd have moved right on.

Her daughter, with whom it would be pointless to argue once she *knew*: Cléo's tale would in no way resemble the testimonies of those who prefaced them with a hashtag: #MeToo.

That of a bad victim, 0.1.

■ ■ ■

She'll be forty-eight years old the day after tomorrow. Lucie and Adrien have been busy for weeks preparing a surprise for her birthday. A big surprise, her daughter specified.

In the sitting room, the computer is still switched on.

A toll-free phone number and an email address— temoignagegalatea-ocrteh@interieur.gouv.fr—have been made available. Alongside the inquiry, another appeal for witnesses has been launched on the Facebook page of the production company ELVENID, *as it prepares to film a documentary on the subject.*

9

orty-eight, that's not a round number, her father objected, when Lucie suggested to him that they organize a birthday surprise for Cléo.

Exactly. She won't be expecting anything special.

Adrien and Lucie were soon in cahoots, sharing intelligence, meeting at the café downstairs on Sunday afternoon, talking Cléo.

Which names still crop up?

Lara. Credit to Cléo, she's never minded, in front of Lucie, describing Lara as her ex-lover, her "great love affair."

Her dresser, Claude, whom she still corresponds with?

And what about the guy whose writings Cléo has kept? The father of that Jonas? Yonach?

When younger, Lucie sometimes half-opened that drawer under her parents' bed, only to be instantly put off by the jumble of notebooks, old magazines, and pages of writing.

Yonasz's parents' phone number, in the 1987 notebook, just rings unanswered, but his work email address was easy to find on the net, the spelling of his first name distinguishing him from the other Varlinskys.

Claude's email address is stored in the digital address book on Cléo's computer. But she doesn't reply to Lucie's message.

As for Lara, Adrien got hold of her email address by contacting the residents' association of the building she still lives in.

10

The first word he says to her, when Cléo opens the door to him, is: sorry. Yonasz is sorry to be thirty-two years and twenty minutes late to her birthday party.

The forty-eight-year-old Cléo bursts into laughter just like the sixteen-year-old Cléo. The forty-eight-year-old Cléo seems to have skirted time, her face that of a former child with bare lashes. Yonasz hands her a wrapped gift—the complete Mylène Farmer CD collection—and an orange folder with slack elastic, from which he pulls a single sheet of paper: Serge wrote this for her, from his hospital bed in 1993. Yonasz had often thought of sending it to her but hadn't dared.

After dinner, all four of them take a walk along the canal; night is feeling its way, a fan of dark blue skimming the red roof of the Théâtre de la Villette.

Lucie and Adrien hang back, at some distance. Cléo gives a little sign in their direction, see you at home, later.

I think I'd like to tell you something

Yonasz listens to Cléo without interrupting her. Then hands her a tissue. The tears on Cléo's cheeks are as colorless as a shower of rain.

From her pocket, she takes a folded-up newspaper article. If I write to them, if I go ahead, will you come with me? she asks Yonasz.

11

T he server on which the Central Office for Combating Human Trafficking discovered the "Galatea" site was under surveillance for months.

The oldest photos were taken with traditional cameras, no doubt in the early eighties; the most recent, from 1994, revealed their digital trail to the investigators. Beneath each image, an obsolete link leads only to deleted files.

It's a site that looks like a catalogue, but you can't tell what they're selling, these rows of anonymous adolescents, on whom just a few clues—a scrunchy, a Casio wristwatch, a Chevignon sweatshirt—give away when the photos were taken.

Some of the girls seem to be stifling the giggles, their eyes wide open, as though amazed at being there. Others adopt the typical pose of models in magazines: chin down, eyes up.

A catalogue of childhoods ended, with bitten and varnished nails, bangs down to eyebrows, teeth braced.

It's a site that Enid, on first hearing about it from her investigative-journalist brother, doesn't imagine will be the subject of her next documentary.

To film students, she's forever saying that she has no method to pass on to them. She knows only this: you must tell the story of what haunts you. And the subjects of documentaries, like those of novels, are screens that mask our unresolved questions. The subject is neither found, nor looked for, you have to allow yourself to hear it, allow it to call out. It's been there forever, a banal splinter under the skin that can be forgotten the way a chipped tooth can, until you run your tongue over it.

The faces on the site tell a silent story, with hidden subtitles, a story that Enid was slow to realize was one that haunted her.

Three months after the site's discovery, the police succeed in identifying one of the faces on it, thanks to a complaint lodged by the mother of one of the young girls in 1991: D., thirteen years old.

D.'s mother is accusing a "Galatea Foundation" of controlling her daughter. But the foundation has neither a postal address, nor any administrative record; in addition, the concept of control was only enshrined in criminal law in 1994, so the case stopped there.

When contacted and invited in by the police, D., now forty-two, agrees to attend; she first consults an attorney, Maître Barrel. Enid's brother has already been in contact with Barrel's assistant over a different issue, and she easily obtains a copy of D.'s statement for him, the case having lapsed.

Enid's brother makes her read it.

In 1991, I was in eighth grade when a girl in my class caused a stir by announcing she'd been selected by a foundation that gave grants to adolescent girls to finance their "dreams." For her, that was a styling internship at a haute-couture house.

I was passionate about horseback-riding, had posters of horses up in my room, and could go riding in summer because it wasn't expensive in Saubusse, where my grandparents lived. Around Paris, it was only for girls who could afford it.

My mother thought it a good idea for me to try my luck;

she didn't like seeing me hanging around, on Saturdays, on the Place de la Mairie de Cergy.

I soon met a woman from the foundation. She spoke of equal opportunities, "Galatea's founding principle"; she thought my plan was exciting. We met on several occasions, we'd have to "strengthen" my file, it all seemed genuine. She gave me a book on the horse-trainer Bartabas, and one Saturday, she took me to the Louvre, I remember the painting by Géricault, Cheval dans la Tempête. *I was captivated, less by how cultured she was than by her attentiveness. She took charge of my file, organized a photo session—that's where the picture on the site came from.*

About ten days later, Cathy phoned my mother: I'd been selected. The next stage would be to convince members of the judging panel. My mother bought me a dress for the occasion, we spoke of nothing else.

Cathy had explained to me that she couldn't be present, owing to "a conflict of interests."

I went there on my own, feeling very intimidated, I rarely went into Paris, and never to the sixteenth arrondissement. There were five judges, men in their fifties. There were also three girls of around my age, but we didn't talk, probably because we were all in competition. One of the judges even proclaimed: "May the best girl win!" *I was transfixed by the grandness of the meal, the waitress who looked like a model, the judges' conversations among themselves, discussing things I knew nothing about: movies, literature . . . The man dealing with my file was seated beside me. I'd prepared a whole pitch, but he questioned me at length on my favorite songs, my friends. It put me at ease. Particularly as he said, several times, that he was by "bowled over" by how mature I was, how sensitive. As he left, he declared that he was "seduced," and suggested to me that we draw up a plan for my future next time: he'd heard about a show-jumping course in*

Vincennes, at Easter. I was ecstatic. The young waitress drove me home. She told me that I'd caught another judge's eye, a movie producer; I didn't want to be in movies, but I was still flattered. As she was setting off, she handed me an envelope: two hundred francs, while you wait for the grant. A kind of advance, she told me.

When I told Cathy about it, she said that, from now on, "my future was in my own hands." I couldn't believe my luck.

The following Wednesday, I was expecting to be tested, for my file to be assessed. My judge explained to me that Galatea practiced "continuous assessment." Everything counted, above all my "maturity." His response was pivotal, I think. He'd told me that he was a doctor, and when he asked if I'd allow him to show me the muscular-tension points on the back, crucial for galloping, I accepted: "maturity" meant me not being wary of everything. We went into a neighboring room, and he gave me an almost medical massage, which reassured me.

The same envelope, the same sum of money.

I thought about him all the time. I was so hung up on not yet having periods, or breasts, no boy at school paid any attention to me, my father only rarely asked after me, and now, an adult found me beautiful. Graceful. I was dying to see him again, I almost forgot about the grant. At school, we all loved movies where an older man "brought out" a young girl, like in Pretty Woman. *I felt cherished.*

Cathy encouraged me going forward, I was "blessed" to have happened upon a judge of that quality, who, what's more, was "crazy about me." It's on the third occasion that . . . The lunch began in the same way, everything was smart and refined, the conversations as much as the food. First he handed me a little package, a gift: Loulou, the perfume by Cacharel, along with a note: "For a future great horse-woman."

I was wearing a fairly short dress, in wool, that he found "adorable," just as he did my way of helping myself to more dessert: it was proof of sensuality, he told me. He spoke at length on the importance of this "sensuality," and the sensuality of horses, too. Gradually, but I no longer know how, he got round to asking me whether I'd ever been aroused by riding a horse. It made me feel very uncomfortable, and he saw that. Straight away, he talked again about the "maturity" requirements for the grant, hoping I'd meet them. I was on the verge of tears but determined not to give in. That was the test.

The waitress took me home without seeming to notice the state I was in. Inside the envelope, there were four banknotes. I tried to tell my mother that something was wrong, but didn't manage to. How could I have told her that, without being forced, I'd performed fellatio on an adult? Just saying the word, "fellatio," was inconceivable. I had no sexual experience.

When Cathy announced to me that, unfortunately, my file hadn't been accepted, I was convinced that it was my fault, without knowing whether I should have said no to the guy or, on the contrary, applied myself to do better and more.

I didn't dare ask the girl in my class who'd introduced Cathy to me whether she'd been through the same thing. I was afraid, if she hadn't, of being called a "slut." If I could've phoned Cathy . . . But I didn't have her number. Her silence confirmed that I'd disappointed her. I believe I had a breakdown.

I was devastated when my mother lodged a complaint a few months later. I was ashamed. And afraid that, because of it, Cathy would be questioned. The police asked me if I'd been the victim of sexual abuse or extortion of money, I replied that I hadn't.

*I don't know what happened to the other girls at the
lunch. They didn't go to my school. For more than twenty
years, I've thought about it: maybe they never had the girls
come back once they'd been used. Or maybe I seemed too
young to them. Or not young enough.*

T he police show D. two photos from the site that can be digitally traced back to 1990; D. recognizes the girl who introduced Cathy to her: F.

F. refuses to attend the interview, she has every right to. She also refuses to meet Maître Barrel, who has decided to build up a case and hopes more recent victims of Galatea will come forward.

Enid's brother sends an email to F., he'd like to meet her, mentions his investigation for a well-known online news site. F. doesn't reply.

Enid tries her luck: she writes to F. that she's a documentary maker, with no link whatsoever to the police or the law. She and her collaborator, Elvire, have already received a dozen or so prizes at various festivals. The Galatea database intrigues them.

Receiving no reply from F., three weeks later, Enid writes again, a simple meeting in a café doesn't commit her to a thing, and she assures F. that she'll only record her with her permission.

If Enid doesn't record her, F. finally replies, they can meet up. But she doesn't have much to say. And absolutely no intention of lodging a complaint.

It was a girl in ninth grade who told me about Galatea. For me, it worked: my judge did write a letter of recommendation to Lagerfeld, he showed it to me. No one in my family circle could have "recommended" me for anything at all. I showed off at school, about my presents, my grant. But I didn't get it. I had my chance, but, as Cathy kept saying, excellence wasn't given to all. Cathy was very stylish. And the lunches were, too. The first time I saw sushi, it was there, in 1990. They spared no expense.

Enid speaks to F. about D.'s statement.

Yes . . . Well. It's an epidemic right now. Moralizing turns even the nicest things into mud. It's easy for D. to make out that she's a victim. She, like me, went to those lunches of her own accord.

Has F., like D., been a victim of sexual abuse?

I wasn't forced to do anything. How could those men have resisted young girls ready to do anything to be noticed? And I'm not traumatized about having sucked that guy off two or three times. After all, I did the same later in my life, with others I thought I was in love with.

But all the same, it's hard to believe that Cathy knew nothing of what went on during those lunches, and F., like D., was thirteen years old . . .

Cathy probably didn't know a thing; she was only interested in beautiful things, in art. She taught me everything, she . . . educated me. I didn't want to disappoint her.

Okay.
Why did F. choose to talk about the grant to other girls? When she knew that there would be few grants awarded? And why to D.?

The blood rushes to her pale cheeks, hits her forehead.

We didn't have the packed schedules kids today have. My parents had neither the time nor the money to concern themselves with my dreams. As long as I brought home a decent report card and would get a reasonable job, that was enough for them. The future, for me, was to try and catch a boy who didn't live in Cergy, and cling on to his dreams.

D. was forever pining for her horses, she missed them, she watched show-jumping on TV . . . I thought she could give it a try. For me, in any case, it was all over, I hadn't gotten it. If helping's a crime . . .

Her anger makes the waiter return, F. fumbles in her coin purse, doesn't want Enid to settle the bill, the marbled redness of her cheeks slowly fades to pink before settling at pale coral. They have been in this café since the early afternoon, lashed to their table as though to a raft, F.'s hands gripping her purse.

Enid asks no more questions. She just listens to her defending Cathy at length, again talking about her "luck," those restaurants, those presents. F.'s account becomes fuller, with different facets, she mentions a lunch where *things really did go a bit far.*

And how, by chance, due to a compulsory remedial class at school on Wednesdays, she'd had to give up going to the lunches.

Cathy was very understanding.

F. hesitates, asks Enid again whether she's recording her. It's all a bit complicated, she whispers.

They both know that, from this moment on, they're off the record: Cathy had indeed offered for her to become her remunerated "assistant."

Recently, it had crossed her mind. What with *MeToo*.

Because it wasn't all rosy during those lunches. I did consider it, telling about it. But I don't have the right—how can I put it? The right story. It's not the right story. Do you understand? No one's going to feel sorry for me with what I have to tell. I'll be judged. That's normal, I wasn't entirely spotless.

As they leave, Enid suggests that they walk a little, F. declines, would rather go home; she almost twists her ankle on the curb, grabs hold of Enid, apologizes, her head's in *a bit of a spin.*

W hen she gets home, before even making her supper, Enid writes the following in her journal:

I was twelve in 1982. I collected posters of Brooke Shields, just as, six years later, I would adore Vanessa Paradis.

I was crafty, and simpered to get more pocket money. A loudmouth in the schoolyard, I quaked at the thought of greeting my parents' guests; I slashed my denim shorts to reveal the tops of my thighs and cried when my mother threatened to throw away my outgrown Snoopy pajamas.

I lied like a pro, and without remorse, I forged my father's signature on my report card, I stole singles records from Prisunic, borrowed Danielle Steels from the library, and folded over pages in *Cosmo* offering "tricks" to go from "sex loser to sex winner." I spent my Sunday afternoons curled up on the sofa, overdosing on variety programs, sugar rushes, and corrosive fizz.

On Monday mornings, I swore I'd attain the purity of an existence devoid of desires, longed to disappear, counted the calories of all that I swallowed, and forced myself to stand stark naked at the open window of my room; I envied the dry coughs of bronchitis sufferers, jumped, feet together, off walls that were too high until I felt the shock of concrete in my ankles. I yearned for physical suffering.

I wept over Rimbaud's death without ever reading his poems, just like I sobbed if a dog died in a movie, I was left reeling on a daily basis. I veered between a sense of time being too short and years too long. I was waiting for something to happen. I watched out for it, that something, ready to devote myself to it. I fell in love with a stray lock on a forehead, a smile in the bus. My cheeks were as flushed as if I had a permanent fever. I was waiting. My diary contained pages of pledges, like that of *going all out* to live an *exceptional* life, with no idea what that would be, apart from *something else.*

Cathy was an invitation to quit the torpor. I would doubtless have loved Cathy with a passion, loved to be her chosen one.

I would have gone to the lunches as to a competition, to be the most chosen of the chosen ones. To honor Cathy's faith in my future. My apprehension would have been eased by the attentions of those men, their questions. They would have confirmed my naïve conviction that I was remarkable, had a "destiny." They would have confirmed what I was already convinced of: my parents didn't know me.

I would have claimed to know the rules of the game, would have tried to live up to that "maturity" praised by the pseudo-judges. The money would have reinforced the feeling of having one foot in the future: a salary, all to myself. I would have closed my eyes and seen nothing but movies, the kind I was crazy about, in which submitting to a man was dressed up as daring and had the face of Kim Basinger in *9½ Weeks.*

Maybe I would have hesitated to "assist" Cathy. But maybe her supremely well-calculated affection would have gotten the better of my reticence. Maybe my fear of being thrown back into my pre-Cathy life would have gotten the better of my hesitation.

E nid and Elvire phone each other two or three times a day, exchange around a dozen text messages, and then have supper together, unless one of them is away.

They discovered everything together: how to write a CV; the orgasm; doing up an apartment; polyamory, during a brief flirtation with it; catching a train at dawn just to see the sea, like in those sixties movies; failure at competitions; and the art of making a soufflé.

Today, nothing's missing from this loving relationship, except sex.

Their love split marked the start of their collaboration.

After listening to Enid's account of her meeting with F., Elvire is sure of it: they've got their next documentary. An affair involving the prostitution of minors in central Paris at lunchtime, with treacherous women and adolescent victims . . . D. would be its heroine. No question they'd find the funding.

Their disagreements, now they're no longer in the "couple" category, are short-lived and only about organization. But that evening, Elvire's words shock Enid.

If D. was a victim of the Galatea system, F. isn't any less so, Enid protests. And it isn't a prostitution story. Prostitution is a transaction between two adults who've reached an agreement. Those kids hadn't *decided* to exchange sex for an internship or a letter of recommendation. They did it so as not to disappoint

Cathy. Because they loved her, and wanted to continue to be loved by her. Cathy had bet on love reducing them to silence. She was right.

And besides, this affair isn't "exceptional," it concerns them, it concerns everyone, anyone.

Did Elvire remember those rumors of harassment surrounding a producer who was showing interest in their films? Did she remember their delight at receiving an email invitation to his birthday party? What did they do? Did they send back a polite refusal? No, they went to it, flattered to be among the "happy few." They said nothing, and contributed to him carrying on. Accomplices.

We weren't sure it was true. He was talking about producing for us, and was certainly the only one at the time, mutters Elvire.

That evening, they both prepare supper in silence, the way one tries to straighten wobbly scenery.

I f this film goes ahead, Enid writes to Elvire later on, when they've each retreated to their respective apartments, it can't be a portrait of a heroine. The way courage and strength are celebrated right now makes people uncomfortable. It's all about "strong women" who "managed all alone" to "pull through." We hold them up as icons, these women who "won't be pushed around," our craving for heroism is that of a society of spectators riveted to their seats, crushed by helplessness. Being fragile has become an insult. So what will happen to those who are unsure? Those who don't pull through, or only with difficulty, without glory? We end up celebrating the exact same values as this government that we boo: strength, power, conquering, winning.

The Galatea system said exactly that: may the best girl win! The Galatea affair mirrors our malaise: it's not what we're forced to do that destroys us, but what we consent to do that chips away at us; those pricks of shame, from consenting every day to reinforce what we decry: I buy things knowing they're made using slave labor, I go on vacation to a dictatorship with lovely sunny beaches. I go to the birthday party of a harasser who produces my films. We're shot through with such shame, a whirlwind that, little by little, bores into us and hollows us out. Not having said anything. Or done anything. Having said yes because we didn't know how to say no.

T hose lunches, in the nineties, that brought together girls and powerful men? *It was common knowledge.*

These are the words of the female producer of a radio show with whom Enid and Elvire are talking about their forthcoming documentary.

Everyone knew about it.

And if those lunches took place for so many years without anyone complaining about them, it's proof that nothing *that* serious went on at them, she adds.

They were ready to ferret around, wade through piles of documents, use ruses to get answers, but it's all there, out in the open. The Galatea labyrinth is no such thing, its every nook and cranny entirely accessible. They were proud to have unearthed an explosive, but those who'd handled it speak of it casually, as of a toy. A toy one can't remember that clearly, except that it was entertaining. The website is testimony to the indifference of those who *saw* it all: overly expensive presents given to young girls who were excited, then devastated, "chosen" to be used and dismissed.

Some days, the faces on her computer screen seem to disdain Enid, the young girls sneer at her: Enid understands nothing about their story. She's much too old. She should leave them in peace: they loved Cathy with a passion, and at least *something* had happened to them.

Having studied them closely, Enid knows a detail of each

girl's appearance that chokes her: the worn collar of a tee shirt, bitten and varnished nails, the crooked teeth of a smile.

We're coming, she promises them, I'm coming.

F ive months after first hearing about Galatea, Enid and Elvire decide to publish the appeal for witnesses on social media sites.

Between 1984 and 1994, you were around twelve years old. You were approached by a woman inviting you to apply for a grant from a "Galatea Foundation."

After an initial selection process, it was suggested that you attend a lunch to meet the members of the judging panel.

We would like to hear your story. Those interested in doing so can participate in a documentary on the Galatea affair. The first meeting will take place on Sunday, January 27 (details below).

By clicking on the link below, you will be redirected to a site that doesn't record IP addresses. So your answers to the questions will remain anonymous. If you don't wish to answer a particular question, move on to the next one.

Every night, apprehension of the imminent meeting wakes Enid up at the same time, 4:40 A.M. As she sits cross-legged on her bed, facing the window, the moon fades into the orange floodlighting of the Gare du Nord, and the dome of the Sacré-Coeur wraps itself in thick clouds. On the floor below, a baby is crying; slowly, the sobs peter out, and Enid remains alone, facing those numbers from the police report: 0.1 and 0.2.

0.1 crafty, in micro-shorts, a loudmouth in the schoolyard, and terrified at the thought of greeting her parents' guests, 0.1 who's *going all out* to live an *exceptional* life.

0.1 malleable, in love with Cathy, who dispenses love on merit.

0.1 dolled up, at the table of those lunches, at the center of debates, and of the battlefield. Who triumphs once, twice, but not the third time.

0.1 proud of showing "maturity," who says neither yes or no, neither O.K. or not O.K., going through the motions without really understanding them.

0.1 who taps on her parents' door, she's thirteen, stammers the start of something, *I think I'd like to say something*, is stopped with a "we'll see tomorrow, go to bed, it's late," and who recloses the door.

0.1 is twenty, she's thirty, she has created a lexicon of silence for herself. The future is blighted.

0.1 an ordinary forty-year-old, quietly devastated at having been 0.1, at having said yes because she didn't yet know how to say no.

0.1 haunted by the fear of having been 0.1, shame never loses its memory, shame has such a long memory.

0.1 bad victim.

0.1 about whom Enid talks constantly, as Elvire points out to her. More than about 0.2, 0.3, 0.4, 0.5.

Who can boast of never having been that, a 0.1? she retorts.

0.1 whom Enid sketches, shades in, rubs out, and draws again.

0.1 who is almost fifty today. A helpful neighbor, dependable sister, generous friend, exemplary mother.

0.1 about whom an attorney explains to Enid that "these particular girls, we call them corporals," of an army of silence, 0.2 0.3 0.4 0.5.

0.1 about whom a police chief tells Elvire that he's learnt to feel sorry for them, because they're never the 0.1 they think they are, the favorites. They're always preceded by another 0.1.

0.1 the little star of her school, whom numerous famous writers, singers, producers, industrialists came across at "lunches" between 1984 and 1992. Who *knew*.

Without forgetting the others, who *saw*: cook, waitress, next-door neighbors.

O n the page of the appeal for witnesses, one hundred and three people said they were "interested" in attending the meeting. Forty-one signed up for it, their first names seeming more like pseudonyms: Antinéa, Natacha, Coppélia, Jo, Buffy.

0.1 might be among them.

Perhaps, but she won't come, Elvire retorts, because she'd have to face up to the others, the 0.2 0.3 0.4s.

Or, Enid counters, she's waited thirty years to be judged, to be punished, or to be forgiven, and to be rid of those numbers at last. She'll come.

F ew greeted each other, two hugged for a long time. One or two sat cross-legged on the wooden floor, leaning against the radiator or the piano. The gaunt face of that one, whom Enid recognizes, shocks her. Another one keeps both coat and scarf on, as though about to leave. And that one, yawning and tapping away on her phone, seems to have ended up here by chance. A woman with hair pulled tight in a pony-tail asks if the man beside her, her "best friend," she specifies, can stay. Several of them are surprised at the venue, a dance hall? They want to know at what time "it" will end. And check that nothing will be filmed or recorded.

The directors promise, explain: this hall was the only one happy to welcome them on a Sunday, for free. To each one, they hand out a sheet of paper: on it, there are two sentences to be completed, this little exercise will help them to get acquainted.

> *Twenty years ago, I:*
> *Thirty years ago, I:*
> Enid throws out, as an example:
> *Twenty years ago, I: cut my hair very short, and my father was sad.*
> *Thirty years ago, I: belonged, at school, to a small group of pupils who organized initiations pranks.*

Fifteen minutes go by, Enid and Elvire wait in the corridor.

When Enid half-opens the door, the women are writing away, concentrating.

She collects the anonymous papers. Asks if they're all happy for their replies to be read out loud.

Some laughter: *Twenty years ago, I believed in orgasms.*

Two, three rounds of applause: *Thirty years ago, I went to an SOS Racism concert.*

Whistles, laughter: *Twenty years ago, I fell for a riot policeman at a demo.*

> *Twenty years, ago I started to lie to my daughter*
> *Thirty years ago, some of us here know what happened*
> *Thirty years ago, and ever since, not one of us owed a thing to Galatea*
> *Thirty years ago, and ever since, I haven't managed either to remember or to forget*
> *Thirty-five years ago, and ever since, I've wanted to ask for your forgiveness*

A woman has interrupted Enid, holding her hand out towards her, sitting up straight like a schoolgirl who knows the correct answer: *That's me.*

Enid recognizes her, the face right at the top of the second page of the site, a snap taken in the eighties.

That's me, she repeats. That's my paper: "*For thirty-five years, I've wanted to ask for your forgiveness.*"

She stands, a ship's figurehead surrounded by a swarm of murmurs, 0.1 or 0.2, she tightens her ponytail with a flick of the wrist, pulls out, from her back pocket, a folded-up piece of paper. The air hums with hundreds of words never uttered.

I'd like to tell you something. To read you a text that . . .

Wait! The woman who's just cut her short rushes forward from the back of the hall, repeating *wait wait*, she vaults over a pile of coats, pushes aside chairs, her hair forming commas right down her back. They're side by side, then face-to-face, the one taking the other's hand, she clutches it, stops her, or maybe she's drawing her closer.

Acknowledgments

Thank you to the dancers and choreographers who were kind enough to give me some of their time: Mié Coquempot, Jean-Louis Falke, Louise Goulouzelle, Christine Hassid, Vlada Krassilnikova, Nathalie Pubellier, and Sophie Tellier.

Thank you to Gwen Boudon, dresser.

Thank you to Philippe Noisette and to Wayne Byars, who took the trouble to steer me towards these fine people.

Thank you to Fabrice Arfi, Vanina Galili, Noémi Gicquel, Clotilde Lepetit, Marianne Pelcerf, Jean-Marc Souvira, Marine Turchi.

Thank you to Marie-Catherine Vacher for her painstaking rereading, thank you to Bertrand Py.

Thank you to Jérémy Laederich for his trailer.

Thank you to Luis Pitiot for the first reading.

Olivier, thank you.